A Widow in Pearls

A Gemstone Mystery

A WIDOW IN PEARLS

A Gemstone Mystery

by MARY E. STIBAL

LEVEL
BEST BOOKS

First edition

ISBN: 978-1-947915-38-1

This book was professionally typeset on Reedsy.
Find out more at reedsy.com

I dedicate this book to the memory of my parents, Robert Stibal and Marian Marley Stibal, who taught their children of the joy that comes from hard work.

Contents

ACT I

Chapter 1

Madeline knew she'd have to be careful that morning at Coda Gems, but then she was always careful around her best customer, Brooke Sears. More or less. The woman had more money than God.

But it was a toss-up if Brooke was a bitch, or just crusty.

And then Brooke showed up, thirty minutes late, in black slacks and tunic, a sable stole around her shoulders even though it was only early November. So Madeline went with crusty. Maybe it was the sable.

Madeline unlocked the glass front door for Brooke, tall and imperious, her ice-white hair pulled back in a chic chignon, her lips shimmering in ruby red lipstick. With eight carats of diamonds on her right hand, she was glamorous even at 8:30 a.m.

The two women shook hands and Madeline said, "Can I get you a cup of coffee?"

Brooke laughed, "No, thank you. I've already had three this morning. If I have another, I'll go into cardiac arrest. Or something."

Madeline led Brooke to the back office of the small, upscale jewelry store in downtown Boston and sat at her desk, Brooke taking the chair across from her. Brooke leaned forward, "So I just had to see you, and in person is always so much better than the telephone, don't you think? Even if it can be quite inconvenient for me. Like today. Anyway, I have an absolutely brilliant idea." She paused. "Which I know you'll never guess."

Madeline ran her fingers through her riot of short blonde hair, not about to hazard a guess. Brooke was the very rich widow of Henry Sears and lived in Boston's exclusive Louisburg Square. Which meant Brooke's definition of a brilliant idea was likely quite different than hers.

Brooke had been Madeline's customer for just over eighteen months, all of them good. Spectacular actually, but the woman was high maintenance. Very.

Brooke continued, "So did I ever tell you I lived in Manhattan a long time ago? In the 60's and 70's?"

"No, you never mentioned that."

Brooke was reserved, in an aristocratic, grating way. Madeline did know Brooke had two grown children, a son and a daughter, and a rich husband who had been a Standard Oil heir, who had died years ago. And that was it. Brooke never talked about herself, much less her family. Which was just fine with Madeline. She had no interest in becoming involved with any customer on a personal level, and that included Brooke Sears.

Brooke toyed with her diamond rings and spoke wistfully. Brooke smiled again. "I knew everyone back then in Manhattan. Well, everyone that mattered. My husband and I owned a co-op just off First Avenue. We were out every night in those days, on the East Side of course, the West Side, the Village. Even Tribeca once or twice. Of course we were invited to Truman Capote's Black and White Ball. I'm sure you've read about it? A party for the rich and the famous, and a couple of people from...Kansas, I think it was."

Brooke sighed and leaned back in her chair.

"Those were amazing times. I even met a couple Black Panthers at Lenny Bernstein's one night. He was anti-war of course. And I knew Betty Friedan, who taught me how to make a spinach soufflé one morning at three a.m. And then there was what's his name with the glasses and the horrible hair, Andy..." A pause and she added, "Warhol. That's it. Warhol. But those days are long gone, as are most of my old friends."

"Well, that must have been quite interesting," said Madeline, wondering where all this was going. At 8:35 in the damn morning.

Brooke nodded. "Of course, most of them were much older than me. But it was an extraordinary time really. Tumultuous. That's a good word, isn't it?" She laughed. "Anyway, I thought I would write a book about those years

4

in Manhattan. A snapshot of the people I knew, and what it was like, back in those days." She paused then said, "Does that surprise you?"

Madeline was not surprised, she was speechless. Brooke Sears writing a memoir? The woman was the most private person Madeline had ever known. And now she meant to write a book about her long-ago, high-octane social life?Maybe it was because Brooke was getting old. That must be it. Maybe she wanted to re-live a happy part of her life because almost everyone she had known back then was dead.

Brooke broke the silence. "You know, Madeline, I will have a cup of coffee. Just thinking about my book makes me want caffeine. It's a good thing I quit smoking thirty years ago or I'd light up a cigarette. I almost wish I had one now." She looked at Madeline as if she might pull one out of her purse and hand it over.

Madeline didn't have a cigarette but she did have a joint in her desk drawer, which would stay there. Madeline went to the coffee maker, punched the brew button and said, "Well, that's great. A book? Really?" Not asking about cream or sugar. Brooke took her coffee black and her martinis extra-dry and straight up.

Brooke laughed, "I won't write about everything of course. No, definitely *not* everything, and *certainly* nothing personal. My private life is not anyone's business. At all. But I was going through some old papers the other day..." Her voice trailed off. "Anyway, I was thinking that a book about the old days in Manhattan would be a fascinating read, written by someone who was there. An observer. That's what I'll be, an eyewitness. Like what's his name, that English writer a couple of centuries ago...."

Madeline hadn't gotten a minor in English Lit for nothing. "Like Samuel Pepys?" Brooke laughed. "Yes, that's his name. How clever of you," she said. "Anyway, I do think my book will make the *New York Times* best seller list, for six months at least. Maybe even a year."

Madeline thought either scenario unlikely, but said, as she set a cup of black coffee in front of Brooke, "Well, yes, that could happen." She paused for a heartbeat and continued, "To be honest, I thought you wanted to talk about buying a new piece of—"

5

Brooke waved a dismissive hand, the one with the diamonds. "I don't have time to think about pearls. Not now. Just my book."

So Brooke hadn't come to buy. Madeline hid her disappointment. She'd hoped to surprise her business partner, Abby, with good news. Their store was on the seventh floor of the aged Jewelers Building, but they had lost their lease, so Coda Gems would have to move to God knew where. Most likely to a not-so-great place, the only kind they could afford. Anxious just thinking about it, she fingered the eighteen-karat gold jeweler's loupe she wore around her neck.

"Yes, it will be good to go back and remember those days," continued Brooke, her pale gray eyes soft for once. She picked up her cup of coffee and set it back down. "The best time of my life. Yes, it was the best."

Madeline knew she should say something supportive, given the 'Best Customer' part, so she did. "Working on your memoir does sound like it would be fascinating. A lot of work, but fun."

"Yes, it will be," said Brooke with a smile. "The good part is I've saved everything, and I do mean everything from those years. My old diaries, invitations, letters, press clippings, that sort of thing. They're organized at least. Sort of. That's why I came to see you. Because I thought you'd want to help." A ruby red smile and then, "We can go through my boxes together, just the two of us for a couple of weeks. Or maybe more. Like you said, it will be fun."

Madeline hesitated. She shouldn't have used the word 'fun.' Brooke's brilliant idea didn't sound like fun, it sounded like a gigantic pain.

Brooke added, almost as an afterthought, "I'll pay you, of course. Whatever the going rate is for a...secretary. I am sure you can check into that. Just let me know." Another smile and, "You see, I do need to work with someone I can trust to go through my boxes with me. Since they're full of personal information, very private information. I can't have just anyone going through..."

Brooke's cell phone rang and she pulled it out of her purse and answered with her standard, imperious greeting. "And?" She listened for fifteen seconds, said "fine," and disconnected, and turned to Madeline. "Yes, it will be great to work with you on my book."

Madeline watched Brooke glance out at Coda Gems' small but elegant retail space, three long, cut-glass cases glittering with eighteen-karat gold, gemstone jewelry and designer watches, and the Impressionist prints on the walls that had cost her and Abby an arm and a leg. Well, the frames had cost an arm and a leg. Brooke looked back at Madeline. Waiting.

After a hesitation, Madeline said, "Well, I can help go through *one* box of your papers and we'll see how it—"

Brooke interrupted, "You know, I don't think it would do to work here since your store is so, well you know, it is small. Tiny really. Not much room. And I definitely do not want the mess at my townhouse since we'll need to spread out my papers. Your place in the Seaport District would be much better for that." Brooke smiled. "Yes, it has a lot of space. Relatively speaking that is."

Madeline made the mistake of nodding at that last part, and Brooke stood up. "Well then, I'm glad we've got that settled. I'll have my papers dropped off at your flat. Sorry, but I have to go. We'll talk." And with that she walked to the front and out the door.

Madeline stared after her. Classic Brooke. Outrageous. The woman was impossible. And it irked her that Brooke always referred to her condo on Channel Center St. as a 'flat.' Brooke had told her once, "it sounds so much better than the pedestrian 'condominium,' don't you think?"

Madeline didn't feel pedestrian. She also didn't feel like working with Brooke on her book, which was now right at the top of her "I'd rather be dead" list.

***

Madeline's business partner Abby Black walked in a few minutes later and Madeline didn't need to check her watch. It would be nine o'clock, exactly. Abby was nothing if not precise. She was in charge of sales as well as their finances and dressed like a CFO, a blue suit under her trench coat, low heels, and a simple gold necklace. Straightforward. Even her hair was sensible, short and glossy black.

Abby said, "I saw Brooke at the elevator so I'm assuming she was here to see you." She looked Madeline up and down. "So that must be why you're so dressed up?"

Madeline ignored the comment. She was in her usual black designer jeans, and given the season, a black cashmere sweater, and cowboy boots, expensive and hand-tooled ones. Today's were candy-apple red.

Madeline said, "Brooke was here, but not to buy. She's decided to write a book about the time she lived in Manhattan. Almost fifty years ago."

"Brooke is writing an autobiography? That seems…out of character."

Madeline laughed. "I know. But not an autobiography. A memoir about the people she knew back then." She arched her eyebrows. "Brooke has decided I'm to help go through her papers."

Abby hung her trench coat in the closet and said over her shoulder. "Really? She asked you to do that?" Abby walked to their small refrigerator and set two plastic-covered bowls inside. Her lunch. Likely a salad in one and soup in the other. Vegetable.

Madeline said, "Well she didn't exactly ask. She took a 'yes' for granted. Seems she and her husband were out every night years ago with the rich and the famous. And now she intends to write about it. With me as her assistant." Abby didn't say anything and Madeline continued, "So I told Brooke I'd go through one box of papers and see how it goes."

Abby sighed, "Helping her out for a bit won't kill you. We need her."

To be precise, they needed Brooke's money.

Madeline knew Abby's dream, since they had to re-locate, was to move Coda Gems to Newbury Street in Boston's Back Bay, twelve long blocks away, a pricey neighborhood of high end-stores, and high-end shoppers. But the Back Bay had rents they couldn't possibly afford, which Madeline had pointed out to Abby the week before. About five or six times more than necessary.

There was an undercurrent of 'testy' now between the two partners.

Madeline added, "Working with Brooke on her ridiculous book will be a huge waste of time."

"It won't kill you," repeated Abby.

Madeline sighed. "I just hate the idea of getting trapped in Brooke's 'observations' about her life in Manhattan. That's how she described this book of hers, as if she were a modern- day Samuel Pepys for God's sake."

"Who's he?" asked Abby not looking up. She was at her desk on her calculator, running their latest sales numbers, the first thing she did every morning.

"Never mind," said Madeline.

Abby, her fingers still flying on the calculator, said, "So why don't you find an executive assistant for Brooke? She might like that since it does sound rather grand. That should keep her happy." A pause as she looked up. "And you."

Abby didn't mention that Madeline had lost a big client of Coda Gems the month before. A major setback, even if it hadn't been her fault. Exactly. Well, to be honest it had been her fault. She could be outspoken, which Abby had said at the time the rich didn't always appreciate.

Madeline stood up. "An executive assistant? I don't think Brooke would be happy with that."

"Well," Abby said, frowning, "satisfied would be good enough. You can at least see what she thinks."

Madeline shrugged. "I can do that. See what she thinks."

"Perfect," said Abby. She went back to her numbers.

It had taken the partners almost a year to work out the division of labor. Abby worked with customers who walked in, with Madeline as back-up. Madeline's main responsibility was as the store's buyer, covering both estate and online auctions, as well as running their ten big retail accounts, like Saks Fifth Avenue. Brooke was Madeline's only regular customer.

Regardless, she knew Brooke would dismiss the executive assistant idea with a slight intake of breath and a furrowing of her perfect, elegant eyebrows. Which meant Madeline would end up working with her on her damn book.

***

9

Madeline walked into the lobby of her building after seven that evening, exhausted from a day of negotiating with New York gem dealers. Abby had handled the few customers that had straggled into the store. The sooner they moved Coda Gems to a great location the better.

Madeline checked her mailbox, stuffed a stack of bills in her purse and headed to the elevator. All she wanted now was a martini, straight up, with a twist.

But the concierge at the front desk stopped her. "A delivery came for you this afternoon."

"A delivery? For me? Thanks. I'll take it up now."

"It's not that easy," he said, and walked her to the back room.

A stack of large moving boxes was jammed into the small space. Madeline didn't need to check the labels. She knew they were from Brooke. The woman really did assume too much. Madeline had thought there would be one small box, maybe two. Arriving in a week or so. But Brooke had sent, and Madeline stopped to count, fifteen. A small truckload. She could hardly send them back.

The concierge said, "I'm happy to wheel them up for you."

Madeline sighed. "Fine." She took the elevator to her eleventh-floor condo.

Fifteen minutes later Brooke's boxes were stacked in her study, covering the entire wall. It looked like she was moving in. Or out. She fixed herself a second martini. She had no intention of sifting through the contents of all these boxes with Brooke. Tomorrow morning she'd go online and pull off the resumes of a couple of good 'executive assistant' candidates. Ones that Brooke might like. And somehow talk her into it.

But that last part didn't happen, because by then Brooke Sears was dead.

***

Madeline heard about the suspicious death of a woman in Boston's Louisburg Square on TV as she got ready for work that next morning. Sad, she thought. 'Life in the Big City' sad. The only surprising part was that it happened in Louisburg Square, the most upscale corner of Beacon Hill. It was the kind of neighborhood where people didn't drop dead, much less suspiciously.

She opened her computer and saw a TV breaking news spot on her screen. "Mrs. Brooke Sears, 73, was found dead in her Louisburg Square townhouse last night. Her death is under investigation by Boston Police as a possible homicide."

Madeline froze. What? They must have the name wrong. Brooke? Dead? But the reporter had no further information. And neither did the other Boston news channels. Her heart racing, Madeline dialed Abby's cell phone.

Abby answered after five long rings. Madeline said in a rush of words, "Brooke, our Brooke, is dead. She was murdered last night at home. At least the police think she was murdered. Whatever, she's dead."

A gasp from Abby. "What? Brooke? I can't believe it. Last night? Murdered? You're sure?"

"It's all over the news."

"How…horrible. What happened?"

"I don't know. The only thing I know for sure is that she is dead. And not from natural causes. I don't know anything else. Nothing. Nada. Bupkis." And then in the silence Madeline added, unnecessarily, "Zero."

Which must have annoyed Abby because she said, "Zero? So what will you do?"

"Do?"

"I mean, what will you do to find out what happened to her?"

"Do? Keep checking the news, I guess."

"Really? That's it? That's the best you can do, check the internet? She was our best customer after all. Your customer."

Madeline muttered through gritted teeth, "I have to go." And she hung up, staring at the phone.

So exactly what was she supposed to do? Madeline still remembered the main number for *The Boston Globe* and punched it in on her phone. Her ex-husband, the second not the first, had been the lead reporter on the paper's Spotlight team of investigative reporters when they were married. But that was a couple of years ago, before Felix had left her and *The Globe* for a job in Chicago. She'd heard he was living with a redhead, now. Younger too.

At the prompt she pressed five for the Spotlight desk, but all she got was a recording, and Madeline didn't leave a message. Felix had won a Pulitzer when he'd been at *The Globe* so of course they would know who he was. But she was not about to introduce herself as his ex-wife, then ask for information about a murder in Louisburg Square.

When they'd been married, Felix told Madeline more than once that the best news source was an insider. But she didn't know the names much less the phone numbers of Brooke's children, and even if she did, she could hardly call them up hours after their mother had been murdered. The second best source he'd said was a contact in the police department. Felix had mentioned a third, but she couldn't remember it.

Which left her only with the second option, the police. She sighed. The only time she'd spoken to a cop was seven years ago when she got a ticket for blowing through a red light in Hull. Still, the Boston police might tell her something about Brooke's death. Enough to keep Abby happy, for now.

***

Madeline left a message for Abby saying she'd be in late, then called the Beacon Hill precinct. She drove to the shimmering stone and glass headquarters of the Boston Police Dept. at One Schroeder Plaza. It took her over twenty minutes to find a parking spot in the jammed lot. She was on the verge of giving up when a girl in a ponytail pulled out of a space with a defiant squeal of tires and Madeline pulled in.

She yanked open the front door and walked into a government-issue reception area, making her way through the usual security scanners. The handsome officer at the looming front desk smiled at her as she approached. So far so good.

"I'd like to speak to the officer in charge of Brooke Sears's investigation. Please."

The officer just stared at her.

Madeline added, "Brooke Sears is, I mean was, a customer of mine, and she came to see me yesterday morning. And I was told that her death...her

12

murder, is being handled here, at headquarters?"

The officer nodded, took down her name, told her to take a seat, and picked up the phone. For thirty minutes Madeline sat alone on their big, cold, wooden bench and watched a stream of Boston citizens walk through the door. They all looked guilty of something. Finally, a slender woman, late thirties, wearing gray slacks and jacket walked up to her like a dancer on the balls of her feet. Her long dark brown hair was pulled back, her voice low.No lipstick. A computer bag slung over her shoulder.

She said, "Are you Madeline Lane?"

Madeline nodded.

"I'm Detective Donia Amick, the officer in charge of the investigation into Mrs. Sears's death. I understand you saw her yesterday?"

Madeline stood up, surprised. She had expected a grizzled, middle-aged man, tired and wrinkled. A hard-eyed cop. Not a beautiful woman with deep brown eyes.

"Yes, I spoke to Brooke."

"Thank you for coming in. I do appreciate it. Please come with me." She led Madeline through a second set of security scanners, her back straight. A prima ballerina type. Which could be good. Or not.

Madeline followed the officer into an elevator that stopped at the second floor. The detective showed Madeline into a spartan room with four chairs, a table, and no windows. Waving her to a chair, Detective Amick sat across from her, and pulled a laptop out of her bag. "Thank you again for coming in. And by the way, our conversation will be recorded, for purposes of accuracy." She asked Madeline for her date of birth and contact information, typed the information, then turned to Madeline. "And how did you know the late Mrs. Sears?"

"Brooke was a customer of mine for over a year at Coda Gems. I'm one of the owners. We're in the Jewelers' Building in Downtown Crossing, and we sell jewelry. Obviously. Brooke came to see me yesterday morning."

Detective Amick glanced at her watch. 'Cartier' thought Madeline. She leaned closer for a better look. It wasn't.

Madeline continued. "I'd like to know how Brooke died...exactly what happened to her."

"My condolences. And what was the reason Mrs. Sears came to see you yesterday?"

"Like I said, Brooke was a good customer," said Madeline, leaving out the 'crusty' part. "But Brooke didn't come to talk about jewelry. She wanted my help in going through old papers for a book she wanted to write. A sort of memoir. She was there for about fifteen minutes, took a call on her cell, then left."

"What time?"

"She left around 8:45."

"And did Mrs. Sears express any concerns about a neighbor, a friend or a relative? Or mention anyone or anything that was bothering her?"

"No, nothing like that," Madeline said. "So, do you have any suspects? Any motive? I...I just want to know what happened. The specifics, if you don't mind."

"Were the two of you close?"

"Do you mean were we friends?" Madeline paused. "Well no. We spent a lot of time together but...friends, no."

"What jewelry, if any, did she usually wear?"

"She wore a diamond engagement ring and a wedding ring, as well as two pearl and diamond bracelets. Every day."

"And what would you say is the approximate value of these jewelry items?"

"I would say about fifty or sixty thousand dollars. Maybe more."

If Amick was surprised by that information, she didn't show it. She asked Madeline to describe the jewelry in detail, which she did.

"Do you know if there was other jewelry she kept in her home?" Detective Amick asked.

"There wasn't. Brooke did have a large collection of pearl jewelry, but for insurance reasons she kept most of it in her safe deposit box at the Bank of America, the one on Federal Street. She took those pieces out only for special occasions."

Madeline knew that for a fact because Brooke had her sign a signature card for her safe deposit box, and would send her at least once a month to the bank to either pick up a piece of pearl jewelry, or return it. It was often enough that Abby once told Madeline she had become Brooke's personal assistant. Which was closer to the truth than Madeline wanted to admit.

"Where did Mrs. Sears keep her jewelry at night?"

"I wouldn't know. Was something stolen?"

The detective didn't answer.

"Like I said," Madeline continued, "Brooke talked about a book she wanted to write, and then said she'd have her old papers sent to my place. She had them delivered sometime yesterday because they were there when I got home from work last night."

"Old papers?"

Madeline nodded. "Yes. She kept old letters and newspaper clippings, that sort of thing. From when she and her husband lived in Manhattan."

"And you have them now?"

"Yes. Fifteen boxes of papers, big ones. Moving boxes actually."

The detective leaned back in an old swivel chair, and Madeline caught a glimpse of the handcuffs hooked on her belt.

Detective Amick said, "I'll want to take a look at these boxes. I'll send an officer to pick them up. They'll call first." The woman hadn't smiled once the whole time. Not that this was a smiley kind of conversation. "What time did you get home last night?"

Madeline froze. She had come to headquarters to find out what had happened to Brooke, not to be questioned herself.

"You're asking me for an alibi?" Madeline asked.

Detective Amick didn't take her eyes off Madeline's. "I'm just looking for information. So what did you do last night?"

Madeline stared back at her. She could hardly refuse to answer. "I drove home at 6:30, had a pizza delivered. And then I watched a movie on Netflix."

"Were you with anyone? A friend maybe?"

"No."

"After you got home did you leave the building again?"

"No."

"What is the make, color and model number of your car?"

15

Madeline gave her the information on her gray Audi. "Why would you want that? I'm sorry, but I am here because I want to know what happened to Brooke. I'd appreciate any information you can give me and the details of her…murder."

Detective Amick sighed. "Since this is an ongoing investigation, I can't provide much information. I can tell you that at 8:15 last night there was a 911 call reporting a loud noise, which may or may not have been a gunshot. Two officers responded. That is all I can tell you at this point. Thank you for coming in. I'll be in touch if I have any further questions."

"So Brooke could have interrupted a robbery in progress?"

"I really can't discuss that." She stood up, and Madeline did as well. So it was likely she'd been shot during a burglary. And ended up dead. It happened all the time. In the movies.

Amick walked Madeline to the lobby. At the front door Madeline looked behind her, and saw the detective staring after her. She'd probably have done better with a middle-aged man, overweight and macho than a ballerina-type cop.

But at least Madeline had shown up, and talked to the police, even if the detective on the case had asked her for an alibi, and didn't seem to like her. Nevertheless, Madeline had done what she needed to do and could give Abby an update.

***

As soon as Madeline left, Detective Amick walked back to her cubicle, neat piles of papers stacked on her desk, a clutch of framed photos in the center. She clicked on her computer and sighed. This case was not a run-of-the mill homicide, but the murder of a prominent and very wealthy Bostonian with political connections. Superintendent Solomon, the head of Homicide was already breathing down her neck, and the case was only twelve hours old.

It was a little odd that Madeline Lane had showed up so soon after Brooke Sears's murder with questions. The detective had met all kinds of people who wanted to talk to police after a high-profile murder. She had two categories, the 'crazies' who simply wanted to connect with the police and get attention, and a second kind, helpful, concerned citizens. There was a third category of course, the murderer, looking to find out what the police knew. Fishing for information. Wanting to know where the investigation was heading. She put Madeline in the second category. But Madeline had pressed her several times for details, anxious to know what the police knew, which meant the woman could perhaps, possibly land in the third.

The detective opened Brooke Sears's folder and scanned the crime scene photos and reports again. Brooke had been shot in her study, and the drawers of her desk as well as those in the bookcase had been pulled out and rifled through. The victim's townhouse did have a security system, but it unfortunately had not been activated the night she was murdered.

Since the police hadn't found any jewelry on her person, it was possible the jewelry that Brooke usually wore had been the motive. And since there wasn't any evidence of a break-in, it would seem that Brooke had let the person or persons inside. Which suggested she knew them.

As a precaution, Detective Amick put out a standard thirty-day pawn store tracker on Brooke's jewelry, listing Madeline's description of her wedding rings and pearl and diamond bracelets. The detective already had Brooke's son Cecil pulling together a list of Brooke's family, friends, and acquaintances. And now she'd add Madeline to that list.

The detective looked at her calendar. Only thirty-seven days before she could transfer out of Homicide to the Special Operations Unit. And it couldn't come soon enough. As a little girl she'd had pink tutus in her closet, but as an adult she preferred camouflage and bullet-proof vests. She had been waiting for over a year for a position in Special Ops to open up.

Donia had been in Homicide for three years and found nothing intriguing about the work, which was pretty much, "The Butler Did It." Even gang-related murders were connect-the-dots. Not exactly challenging. She found homicide cases to be boring. Tacky, bloodstained, and boring. This case might be different. But more likely not. She called Officer Baxter and told him to drive over to Madeline's building and have the manager download a file from the last ten days of the garage security camera onto a flash drive. She gave him Madeline's phone number to arrange for pick-up of Mrs. Sears's boxes.

Detective Amick wrote up her interview with Madeline and emailed a copy to Superintendent Solomon, who showed up at her cubicle an hour later, leaning over the partition. He never sat in the chair by her desk. He wasn't the sitting down type.

"Well," he began, "I've got bad news and worse news. Which do you want first?"

"I'll take worse," she said. "Get it over with. Then we can move to the merely bad."

The superintendent laughed, a grim cop laugh. "Well, I'm sorry, but worse and bad are all sort of wrapped up together. There's a chance your transfer won't happen. At least not for a while."

"What?" Detective Amick shoved back her chair and stood up, knocking a stack of folders from the edge of her desk onto the floor. "It was approved two months ago. Everything was all set, you said it was—"

The superintendent interrupted, "Sorry. Here's the worse news. You've got a month to solve this Sears murder or the open slot in Special Ops goes to a Timothy Christison, an Afghanistan vet. I just got the word from Zeus this afternoon." The superintendent always called Commissioner Maxwell "Zeus," although never when he was in earshot.

"But...you promised..."

The superintendent interrupted again. "I know I did, but it's out of my hands now and there is nothing I can do. The mayor must have read Zeus the riot act or something this morning because he's got a hair up his ass on this one. And I am sorry. So solve it already." He managed a tired, apologetic smile. "Let me know if you need anything."

He wheeled around and walked away.

Seething, Detective Amick went back to Brooke's file. She'd need to talk to the woman's son Cecil and make sure he'd get her that list of Brooke's relatives and friends by the end of the day. And then she'd have to shake down her sources, hard, and bring in the usual burglary and home invasion suspects.

Looking for dots to connect.

***

The next day, Brooke's murder made the front pages of *The Boston Globe* and *The Boston Herald*. Madeline read the articles about the murder in both papers five times. Other than mentioning that Brooke had died of a gunshot wound and her death officially classified as a homicide, there was no other information about the crime itself. Most of the articles were devoted to background on Mrs. Sears, complete with her patrician lineage, which to Madeline was a waste of ink. After all, it was unlikely the Daughters of the American Revolution had gunned her down.

***

At 8:15 am, Madeline got a text message from a Police Officer Baxter that he wanted to pick up Brooke's boxes, and she texted back that 4:00 Saturday afternoon would be fine. She had already told Abby she'd spoken to the detective in charge of Brooke's murder, and repeated the little information she'd gleaned. Abby had only said, "How sad that Brooke died because of her jewelry." She seemed unimpressed with Madeline's 'gung-ho, grab 'em by the horns trip' to police headquarters. Which Madeline realized now had been a mistake. She should never have gone to the police.

Madeline folded up the newspapers and walked into her study, staring at the stack of Brooke's boxes. Each had large white stickers with the year scrawled in bold red. The story of Brooke's life in Manhattan all boxed up, neat and tidy, the best years of her life she'd said. Madeline remembered Brooke mentioned she had been at Truman Capote's Black and White Ball. Curious, Madeline went to her computer and googled it. And five hundred thousand links popped up. She knew Capote's long-ago party at the Plaza Hotel in New York was famous, but hadn't realized it was half-a-million-links famous. She checked the date of the ball, Nov. 28, 1966. Had Brooke really been to that super-famous party? Maybe. Madeline had an easy way

19

to find out. She dragged down the box with the 1966 sticker and set it on her desk.

Inside was a row of file folders, arranged alphabetically by last name. No surprise that Brooke had organized the history of her life. The first folder was marked "Agnelli, Gianni & Marella," which would be the super-rich head of Fiat and his upper-class wife. A princess, if she remembered her celebrities correctly. She flipped through the files until she found a thick one, labeled *Capote, Truman* and pulled it out.

Like Brooke said, she had saved everything. Inside were cards and letters from Capote, chatty ones, about lunches or diners, or weekends in the Hamptons. A cruise along the Turkish coast was mentioned in one letter. And then she found Brooke and her husband Henry's invitation to Capote's ball, and about twenty newspaper articles that reported on the event, including five from *The New York Times* alone. She pulled out a stack of photos, the one on top was of Brooke standing in a doorway, dazzling in a long white caftan and ropes of pearls, holding a white swan mask, and next to her a man in a black tux wearing a mask. Likely her rich husband. Madeline flipped through the rest of the pictures of Brooke at Capote's ball, a couple more pictures with her and the masked man, and then one with just her and Capote. She'd forgotten how short he was. Then there was a photo of Brooke dancing with Prince Radziwill, although she knew who it was only because Brooke had written his name on the bottom. The last was a picture of Brooke dancing with Frank Sinatra. Sinatra? So Brooke knew him too?

This actually was all quite interesting, and she felt a flash of regret. Going through these papers with Brooke would have been fun. She shoved the file in the box and heaved it back on the stack, then called Abby.

"I'm having a dozen red roses sent to the church on Friday for Brooke's funeral. From both of us."

"Perfect. What church?"

"Trinity Episcopal, in Copley Square," Madeline said. "Can't get any more upper class than that."

"So I assume you'll be going? To her funeral?"

"Me? Go to Brooke's funeral? No. It will just be family and her friends. I won't know anyone there."

Abby sighed. "Madeline, it's not like it's a party. You should definitely go. And I should too. She was a very good, loyal customer. We have to go, both of us. It's the right thing to do."

After a long moment Madeline said, "Well, alright then. Fine. So I'll go."

"We'll close the store for the morning," said Abby, and hung up.

As Madeline got ready to leave for work, she thought about Brooke, who used to call her about something or other at least once a day.

***

Just the month before Brooke had called Madeline and asked her about an Art Deco jewelry sale coming up at Skinner Auction in Boston.

"I told you about that auction three weeks ago," Madeline said. "You said you'd think about it."

"I did? I must have forgotten. I'm looking at a couple of photos now on their website. There are two pearl necklaces coming up, both of them gorgeous. One of them has an emerald clasp. Too bad it's not diamond."

Madeline checked her calendar. "The preview is on Wednesday at one. Do you want to go?"

Brooke said, "I'll be ready at twelve-thirty."

Madeline always drove Brooke to previews or auctions she felt like attending. It was part of the job.

"No problem," said Madeline.

So that Wednesday Madeline double-parked in front of Brooke's townhouse at half past twelve, left the engine running and called Brooke's cell. "I'm out front," said Madeline when Brooke picked up.

"Good."

But ten minutes later she hadn't come out so Madeline called again. This time there was no answer, her call going right to voice mail. What on earth was Brooke doing? She must be on the other line. Or something. The woman was always late. Annoyed, Madeline leaned on the horn. A couple of times. Another five minutes passed before Brooke swanned down the front steps in a slim black suit with a nipped waist. Probably Chanel. From a distance, she looked like a 1950's runway model.

"That was inappropriate," Brooke said as she slid into Madeline's car. "Did you really need to do that? I mean really."

"You mean honk?"

Brooke glared at her. "Yes. That was tasteless."

"You were late."

"Don't do it again."

"I'll try," said Madeline, and zoomed down the street, making an illegal right turn at a red light. Brooke glanced at her but didn't say anything.

***

Later that afternoon Detective Amick still didn't have any dots to connect. She spent an hour on her computer fast-forwarded the grainy, flickering images from the surveillance camera outside the garage of Madeline's building. They showed Madeline driving into the garage at 6:07 pm, the night of Brooke's murder. But Madeline's car hadn't left the garage again until the next morning at 7:55.

The detective had already talked to her best snitches, gang and otherwise, who'd all claimed they had heard nothing about the murder of Brooke Sears, although they lied as often as they told the truth. She had nothing to go on, not even a glimmer of a lead. Well she did have a bullet, but that was it.

So where were the woman's damn boxes? She called Officer Baxter but he didn't pick up. She left a stinging message that she wanted those boxes out of Madeline's residence pronto.

Detective Amick went back to Madeline Lane's statement. Nothing there either except…a tantalizing thought. This Madeline did know what jewelry the victim kept in her townhouse, over fifty thousand dollars worth. Interesting. But Madeline couldn't have shot the woman and then robbed her that night, unless…unless she hadn't driven her car out of the building but had perhaps left on foot? Maybe taken a cab to the victim's residence, or had an accomplice waiting?

The detective called the manager at Madeline's building, and was told yes, someone could have taken the elevator to the garage and left through a side door in the back. It was the only door in the building that wasn't monitored by a camera.

Which meant Madeline as a suspect was a possibility, and the only real suspect she had. Amick decided a bit of surveillance couldn't hurt. She called Officer Baxter and in a short, sharp message told him to set up surveillance on Madeline Lane. After she hung up, she wished she hadn't used the word 'pronto' again, but she needed something to happen. Fast.

Chapter 2

The day of Brooke's funeral was dismal and overcast, which Madeline thought was appropriately sad weather for a final farewell, even if the woman had been a demanding, acerbic, pain-in-the-butt.

Madeline had been to a number of Old Money Weddings, but never to an Old Money Funeral. It would most likely be the same people, just different smiles. As she walked up to the church, she saw Abby on the top step in a blue raincoat, her matching umbrella at the ready.

A cluster of mourners hurried past her up the steps and rushed inside, just as a glossy black hearse pulled up in front followed by a string of stretch limos.

She nodded to Abby and they walked through the front door and into the vestibule, a waft of incense drifting out as Madeline swung open the doors into the church. Madeline looked around. She'd been right. She didn't see anyone she knew until she spotted Detective Amick in a long, beige coat and no hat, standing against a wall. Her cool brown eyes observant. Of course, there'd be a cop at the funeral, since the deceased was the victim of murder. An important, unsolved murder. A stocky man in a black overcoat walked up to Amick, and they spoke for several minutes. So make that two cops at Brooke's funeral. Detective Amick looked up, her glance skimming across her and Abby, a tightening of the cop's eyes the only sign of recognition.

Madeline was glad she'd finally connected with Officer Baxter about Brooke's boxes. He'd asked how many there were, and when Madeline said fifteen, he'd said he'd send a van at four the next day. Which was good. Madeline wanted them gone.

She and Abby took a seat in a pew well back from the family. Madeline looked around and guessed about three hundred people had settled in the pews, all well dressed, most wearing black. The organ dirge began a minute later and everyone stood as the pallbearers wheeled Brooke's gilded bronze casket up the aisle. Expensive no doubt, but she knew Brooke would have hated the gilded part.

A tall, striking-looking man walked behind Brooke's casket, his long black hair slicked back. He had piercing eyes, and was in his late forties, Madeline guessed. He wore a dark blue linen coat and matching suit, both designer for sure. He must be Brooke's son. A red-haired woman was on his arm. Beside them was a rail-thin woman, no doubt Brooke's daughter. She had spiky black hair, bright red lipstick, a short, black dress, and stiletto heels. Mourning with an edge.

A clutch of over twenty others in varying shades of black followed. The rich relatives.

Brooke's funeral service began when a tall man in black-and-red vestments emerged from the sacristy, a bishop according to the memorial card. He read a string of sad prayers and then the choir sang more hymns, but Madeline's only thought was that Brooke would have approved of the service, impressive and stately, but not overdone. Although a thin splash of gold on the edge of the bishop's vestments wouldn't have hurt.

She glanced around. Detective Amick was now sitting five pews behind. Staring at her. Madeline turned back to the front.

Madeline was right that the dark-haired man was Brooke's son Cecil. At the lectern, he gave a powerful eulogy to his mother, about how much she'd inspired him, and how much he would miss her. The black-haired woman, Brooke's daughter Paige, followed with her own eulogy, shorter and not as sad. There was more organ music and prayers and then the service was over.

Madeline stared at Brooke's coffin as the pallbearers guided it back down the aisle. As it passed their pew, Madeline whispered "Goodbye Brooke."

To be honest, as a final farewell it didn't seem like much.

She remembered when she'd first met Brooke, early one morning, at the Jewelers' Building well over a year and a half ago. She had ended up in Coda

Gems' doorway, lost, limping, and annoyed.

Madeline smiled at the memory.

***

"Well, this is a horribly managed building," Brooke had snapped that day when Madeline buzzed her into the store. The older woman wore a green jacket and matching slacks, and one shoe, the other held in her hand. "This building should be shut down. The whole place. Seriously. I'm looking for Melvin White Gems. The directory in the lobby says his shop is on the seventh floor but I've walked up and down the hallway three times. Maybe four, I stopped counting. I was here to see him three months ago, but he and his shop have apparently disappeared. Vanished. Not anywhere. Disgraceful. On top of that, I twisted the heel of my shoe on one of the cracked tiles out there. I could have fallen and ended up with a concussion. Or a broken hip for God's sake."

Madeline shrugged. "Melvin died a month ago." Brooke just stared at her. "Why don't you sit down for a minute. Have a cup of coffee? Maybe I can do something about your shoe. I am pretty handy with a jeweler's hammer."

"Melvin died? At the very least his business should have sent out a notice to his customers. How inconvenient." Brooke quickly added, "I mean how inconvenient for his family. Very sad of course."

"I expect so." Madeline nodded to the shoe in Brooke's hand, "Your shoe?" And pointed to their Keurig machine in the corner. "Make yourself a cup of coffee while you wait. Starbucks."

Brooke began, "I don't have time for…" but stopped when Madeline shot her a look. Brooke handed her the shoe. Madeline ran her fingers over the gleaming alligator skin, and went in the back office to her workbench. She rummaged through a drawer of diamond and gold testers, extra loupes and millimeter gauges, and grabbed a small jeweler's hammer. She pried off the shoe's short nails and hammered the heel and sole together in less than three minutes.

She walked back to Brooke with the mended shoe. "Likely won't last long, but at least it will get you from here to there. So long as there is not that far away." Madeline added, with a grin, "I shoe horses as well. On the side of course."

Brooke laughed as she slid on her shoe and stood up. "It's perfect." She walked over to the coffee machine. "And you know what, I will make a cup of coffee. And then, if you don't mind, I'd like to look around."

By the time Brooke left thirty minutes later, she had a Cartier watch from Coda Gems on her wrist. Seven thousand dollars' worth of Cartier.

Brooke had come back the next week and bought a pearl necklace and matching bracelet. A month after that she went with Madeline to a Sotheby's jewelry auction in Boston and spent $90,000 on another pearl necklace.

Madeline knew she'd been lucky to have met Brooke. Too bad she was dead.

***

Madeline and Abby filed out of the church and into the vestibule. Brooke's children Cecil and Paige were at the head of the receiving line, saying a few words to each mourner. After ten minutes in the line, Madeline and Abby were in front of the siblings. Madeline introduced herself and Abby. "We are with Coda Gems here in Boston and we are sorry for your loss. Your mother was a very good customer of ours, and we want to let you know how much we appreciated her. She was one of kind, and we will always remember her."

Cecil smiled and said, "Thank you for coming to our mother's service." He added, "There is a reception after at the Ritz, second floor. We hope you can come." Cecil's eyes were gray, penetrating, so like his mother's. His smile was like hers too. Reserved.

Then he and his sister Paige, tears running down her face, turned to speak with an older man with long salt-and-pepper hair and rimless glasses standing off to the side. Madeline and Abby went out the front door of the church, a low roll of thunder signaling rain. Madeline glanced at the clumps of family standing on the steps, wishing she could have spoken longer to Cecil and Paige. She looked around, seeing no sign of Detective Amick. Too bad. She meant to get an update on Brooke's murder investigation before Abby asked her. Again.

Abby glanced at the lowering sky, popped open her umbrella, and said, "Are you going to the reception?"

Madeline shook her head. "To the reception? No. But I wished I had said something more to Cecil and Paige. More than just, 'I'm sorry for your loss.' Such pat words. Ordinary. Superficial really."

Abby shrugged. "So send them sympathy cards tomorrow and write a heartfelt note or something. Anyway, I need to get back to the store." She headed off down the sidewalk.

A minute later Madeline watched Cecil walk out of the church, followed by Paige. They went down the steps to the sidewalk and over to the hearse. Madeline started down the stairs toward them, but at that moment, the funeral director walked up to Cecil.

Not the time to interrupt. Madeline set off for her car, glad that she'd at least said goodbye to Brooke, and had spoken, even if briefly, to her son and daughter. She felt a sense of closure. She'd met her responsibility to Brooke's memory, and she could move on now.

Once in her car, pulling onto the street, she checked her rearview mirror and noticed a brown Nissan two cars behind. It looked like the same car that had been behind her after she'd left the parking garage of her building on her way to Brooke's service. Not that she normally would have noticed the brown car, but after all her best customer had been a murder victim.

Must be just an odd coincidence.

***

Cecil stood next to Paige, watching as their mother's casket was wheeled up to the back of the hearse. It was a surreal moment. He looked away. All he wanted was for the day to be over. Cecil ignored a crush of cousins standing in silence beside the hearse, their umbrellas open against the odd sprinkle.

He felt like he was in a movie.

He hated movies.

Annoyed, Cecil whispered to Paige, "You should have come right away. Not wait until the last minute to show up."

Paige didn't look at him. "You told me that yesterday, and again this morning. I came as soon as I could."

Cecil stared at Paige. For the last ten years, ever since a nasty divorce, she had been absorbed by her so-called career as a film producer. It was a waste of time, and money. In silence, they watched the undertakers slide Brooke's casket into the hearse and swing the doors shut. Cecil checked his watch.

Paige said, "And it wasn't at the last minute. I was here before Mother's wake last night. Eight hours before, Brother Dear."

Cecil snapped, "I've told you not to call me Brother Dear. You could have come earlier, if you'd wanted to. But you didn't. All for another one of your money-down-the toilet movies."

Paige glanced up at the sky and then back to Cecil. "I told you three times I had two investors flying in from Japan. And it took me months to set that up. But it turned out they decided not to put up any..." Her voice trailed off.

"Still, you should have come, right away or at least earlier than you did, and helped with the details."

Irritated, Paige said, "And do what, exactly? You probably had one of your assistants handle everything. Now that I think about it, I'm sure you did. Besides, what else was there for me to do? Solve her murder? What did you want me to do, whip out a magnifying glass? Someone killed Mother, looking for jewelry or money, for drugs most likely. I have financial obligations you know."

Cecil took out his cell phone and clicked it off mute. Jaw clenched, he said, "Of course Paige, how could I have forgotten about your financial obligations? I heard your last movie lost over two million dollars. If it wasn't for Father's money you wouldn't have a career at all. Such as it is. And the movie before that, wasn't that one a financial disaster too?"

It annoyed him that Paige thought of herself as the next Quentin Tarantino. She wasn't. Her independent films were bloodier and more violent, if that was possible, but all of them had been box office bombs. Or so he'd read. He'd seen her first movie and that was more than enough. He hadn't bothered to watch the others.

Paige leaned toward him, too close, but he didn't back up. She said, her lips a slash of red, "My last movie got great reviews at Sundance, and Toronto, and other film festivals." Her voice rising, she added, "But you? You're just a figurehead at father's old law firm."

Cecil turned away.

Paige went on. "If it weren't for his name you wouldn't be a partner, such as it is, at Sears, Taylor & Yost." The last part she said in a loud singsong.

The cluster of cousins by the hearse glanced over.

Cecil ignored her. His law career was just fine. In fact, it couldn't be better, but Paige never read anything except *Variety*. After years of high-profile white-collar trials, and high-profile not guilty verdicts, he was now the most prominent litigator in New England, and had just been short-listed for a vacancy on the Federal Court of Appeals for the First Circuit. A very big deal nomination he was sure to get, assuming all went well in the vetting process. Every family has skeletons, but some families have bigger skeletons than others.

Like his.

So the less Paige knew about his nomination process the better. The good part was she would probably fly back to Los Angeles in a day or so. He glanced over at a group of his mother's friends, all in their seventies, with tasteful glints of eighteen-karat gold. Not like his mother, who, to be honest, had swanned around like a duchess in ropes of pearls.

He turned back to her, managing a thin smile. "I'm sorry, Paige. All I'm saying is that you might just be wasting your time, and most of your trust income making indie films. That's all."

Paige said, her voice low but tight, "You don't know what you're talking about. The script for my next movie is finished. And has a great plot. There's a chance I can get a first look deal with Netflix, and yes, they are that interested. They want another meeting in a couple of weeks. This film will be my big break. Finally. Believe me, it will happen this time."

Believe her? She was a pathological liar, which was the least of her problems.

The rain began falling in earnest and Paige opened her umbrella. "Do you know when Alfred will meet with us and go over Mother's will? I left him a message yesterday but he hasn't called back. I need to know exactly what's in it. As soon as possible."

Alfred was a lawyer, and trustee of the Sears's family trust. It sounded to Cecil like Paige needed money. Again. Some things never change. He said, "So how much of your trust income have you already burned through this year?"

Paige rolled her eyes but didn't say anything. All of it, or close to it he guessed. "I just want to know what's in Mother's will, and I don't want to wait forever. I know you can find out. Alfred," she said, "doesn't like me."

That was putting it mildly. Alfred, who'd worked with Brooke for over thirty years, was uneasy around Paige, and with good reason. He knew what she was capable of. Cecil muttered, "Fine, I'll talk to Alfred and see what I can find out."

"Her will won't need to go through probate though, right? It can be settled right away?"

"Correct. That's how she had Alfred set it up."

The funeral director walked over and said to Cecil, "Sorry to interrupt, but we need to leave for the cemetery now if we're to stay on schedule."

Ignoring Paige, Cecil strode to the first black limo behind the hearse, his wife following behind. He pulled open the door for his wife, and as soon as she was inside, slammed it shut. Although since the limo was a heavy Cadillac the sound was more of a thud than a slam. He went around the limo and got in. As they drove off, he turned to look out the back window, Paige glaring after them.

Cecil would be happy to talk to Alfred about moving up the meeting, especially if it meant getting rid of Paige sooner. He wanted her out of Boston. Forever would be good.

***

In the limo, Cecil took his wife's hand, stared ahead at the backs of the three burly motorcycle cops leading Brooke's funeral procession. They led the hearse through downtown Boston traffic and across the Massachusetts Avenue Bridge to Cambridge, and then to the Mt. Auburn Cemetery, where five generations of Sears were buried.

As they pulled through the gates of the Gothic cemetery, Cecil called Superintendent Solomon, head of the Homicide Unit, but he had to make do with an assistant.

"This is Cecil Sears, and Robert is an old friend of mine. My mother is Brooke Sears, and I stopped by her townhouse this morning but it's still an active crime scene. Which is a problem since I need to get in as soon as possible. Late tonight or first thing tomorrow morning would be perfect."

Cecil heard a shuffling of papers in the background, and the assistant said, "Unfortunately you can't have access today, since they are still processing the scene. I'm not sure when that will be completed."

Cecil said, "Well then I need to see the superintendent right away."

A pause and then, "As it happens, the superintendent will be in the office tomorrow, and he can see you at one. For fifteen minutes."

Cecil thanked her and disconnected. He hated to wait. He stared out the window as the funeral procession drove down the cemetery's narrow graveled lanes, past looming mausoleums and graying tombstones. Finally, the hearse pulled up beside the Sears's family plot and a large green awning. Cecil straightened his tie and stepped out of the limo, brushing away the tears in his eyes.

Cecil watched Paige emerge from the limo behind them, but she ignored him and picked her way to the bishop waiting at the head of the grave, her stiletto heels sinking into the grass. She stood beside him, like it was a photo op.

As a stream of limos with relatives pulled up, Cecil walked over and stood on the other side of the bishop. He rocked back and forth on his heels. Well, this part of his mother's funeral would be over in fifteen or twenty minutes. Then he'd just have to get through the reception, and this horrible day would be over.

And tomorrow, well tomorrow he'd know when he could get in his mother's townhouse.

***

Half an hour later Madeline walked into Coda Gems and stared out their one window to the back of an aged brick building across the alley. It was an historic brick building, but nonetheless a tacky view. But where could they afford to move to? At least Abby hadn't brought up re-locating to Newbury Street. Now that Brooke was dead Abby had to know that dream was gone.

At her desk, Abby looked up and said, "Any news on Brooke's murder?"

Madeline sighed, "No, nothing new."

The buzzer rang and Abby walked out to the front of the store, Madeline staring after her. Brooke had been Madeline's customer after all, but now it seemed that at least according to Abby, she was the keeper of all information on Brooke's death. So to keep Abby happy, Madeline picked up the phone and dialed Detective Amick.

"Hope I'm not interrupting," she began after the detective answered, "Homicide," just like on TV. Madeline continued, "This is Madeline Lane. I'm just following up to see if there is any update on Brooke Sears."

A pause before the detective said, "There is nothing new."

"Nothing new? No suspects?"

"I said there is nothing new. Homicide investigations can be complicated, and require a lot of legwork. Let me assure you we are following up every lead. By the way, how long had you known Mrs. Sears?"

"About a year and a half. Why?"

At that point someone must have walked into the Detective Amick's cubicle because she said, "I have to go, but I will have more questions. I'll be in touch." Then she hung up.

Madeline walked to the front of the store where Abby was re-arranging their diamond bracelets and said, "I just talked to the officer in charge of Brooke's murder and there's nothing new. And by the way, she talks to me like I'm a suspect or something."

"What? Who?"

"The cop in charge of Brooke's murder, a woman, who is asking me all

33

kinds of questions."

"You worry too much. The police will find the burglar, a low-life recidivist, I'm sure. Along with a smoking gun."

"Maybe. But she did ask for an alibi when I showed up that morning after Brooke was murdered. And she just asked a minute ago how long I'd known her."

"That's what detectives are supposed to do, ask questions and get background."

Madeline wanted to point out to Abby she might not have been questioned if she hadn't gone to the Boston police right after Brooke's murder, looking for information. Which had been Abby's idea. But Madeline said nothing. Besides, that wasn't exactly what Abby had suggested, but close enough.

And now she was personally involved in Brooke's murder investigation. She'd have to figure out a way to get un-involved.

***

The next day, Saturday, just before two, Madeline's phone rang. The caller's voice was hurried. "Madeline, this is Cecil Sears, Brooke's son. We spoke briefly at Mother's funeral. Anyway, I just spoke to a detective with the Boston Police and she mentioned your name. Can I stop by? Now? For a few minutes."

"Now?"

"I won't be long. It's important."

"Fine then."

"Thank you, I appreciate it. I'll explain when I see you. What is your address?"

Fifteen minutes later the concierge at the front desk called and said, "Cecil Sears is here to see you."

"Send him up."

By the time she ran a comb a through her hair a couple of times and opened her front door, Cecil, in jeans and a gray suede jacket, was walking around the corner in a rush. He was intense, distracted, his gray eyes sweeping around her condo.

"How nice to see you, Cecil. Come in. Again, my sympathies." He must have breaking news on Brooke's murder. Why else would he stop by?

He said with a tense smile, "Sorry to just show up."

Madeline shrugged. "No problem."

She led him to her sunny kitchen and he said no to coffee. They sat at the counter and Madeline began, "Your mother's service was lovely."

"Thank you. It was kind of you to come to her funeral." He leaned forward. "A detective mentioned my mother had a number of boxes with her personal papers dropped off here, with you, the day she died."

"Yes, she did. The police are coming to pick them up today, at four."

Cecil said, "Yes, I know. The detective told me that too. So if you don't mind, I'd like to take a quick look before they're taken away. I want to make sure my mother didn't accidentally stuff a big envelope of old estate records in one of them. I saw the envelope on her desk the morning she died, but I can't get back in her place until Monday, and I just want to make sure she hadn't stuffed it in one of her boxes..." His voice trailed off.

"An envelope?"

"Yes. A big manila envelope, with old papers inside. I stopped by her townhouse while the police were still there and they let me stick my head in the door, but I didn't see the envelope on her desk. Anyway, I would really, really appreciate it if I could go through her boxes before the police pick them up. I promise to be quick." He said the last with a wry smile, his gray eyes so like Brooke's Madeline had to look away. "I'm concerned the police might keep her papers for months. So I'd just like to check."

Madeline said, "Well, I guess that's fine. There's quite a lot of them though." She walked Cecil into her study with its wall of cardboard boxes.

He counted them twice. "Is this all of them?"

She nodded and said, "Yes."

Cecil smiled, running his right hand through his long dark hair. "I can't believe she kept all her letters and papers for all these years. Which is good, of course. The Boston Public Library will be pleased. As soon as I get everything back from the police, I'm donating her papers to the library, for their Sears's

Family Collection."

Startled, Madeline spun around and faced him. "What? Cecil, you can't be serious. You want to turn your mother's private papers over to a public library?"

"Yes. That's what I've decided."

"But that's ridiculous. You can't do that." She hesitated and added, "I mean you really shouldn't do that."

He said, irritated, "I didn't come here to discuss the disposition of my mother's personal papers. I'll go through them thoroughly once I get them back, but I've decided that's where they belong. You know my family donated the money to build it in 1895 and..."

"Well, bully for them. But that doesn't mean you should just turn over years of her papers to a...a public library of all places. Brooke would hate that. I mean she would really hate that."

Cecil checked his watch. "I appreciate your concern, but my mother planned to write a book about her years in Manhattan, so privacy was obviously not a worry. The library already has Sears's family papers that go back five generations. Which by the way they consider a valuable historical resource."

"But Cecil, she was going to write about people she knew, not about her personal life," she snapped.

Cecil shrugged. "Like I said, I won't be long, but I do need to go through them. All of them, I do appreciate your patience."

Madeline waited, watching him as he counted the boxes against the wall again. Cecil said, "So if you don't mind, I'll get started."

He seemed to have missed the fact that she hadn't agreed to anything, but she bit her tongue. The man had just buried his mother after all. Cecil pulled one of the top boxes from the stack, and started to flip through the folders as Madeline stood in the doorway. He looked up and commented, "I don't mean to hold you up."

"You're not." She went to the desk in the corner and clicked on her computer, one eye on Cecil.

After twenty long minutes of sifting through the boxes, Cecil broke the silence. "My mother really did keep everything from back then, didn't she?"

Madeline looked up, gave him a frosty smile, and went back to her computer.

Ten minutes later, he finished with the last box and set it on the floor. "You're sure this is all of them?"

Madeline said, not hiding her annoyance, "Cecil, for the last time, yes. Every box she had delivered is here, in this room." She rummaged in a desk drawer and pulled out a pink form. "This is from the delivery company. For fifteen boxes," and handed it to Cecil. He glanced at it and slid it in his pocket.

"So you didn't find that…envelope or whatever it was you were looking for?"

"No," he said, looking at the stack of boxes. "It isn't here." He drummed his fingers on a box. "I thought it might be. But it isn't, so it must be somewhere at Mother's place. At least I know for sure it isn't here." He grabbed his jacket. "Thank you, and I apologize for any inconvenience."

She led him to the door, and after a hurried handshake, he headed to the elevator.

Madeline waited a minute, went to her living room window, and watched Cecil stride to his Land Rover illegally parked in front of her building. The man certainly had a sense of entitlement. Maybe she shouldn't have let him go through the boxes? Although no harm done, since he hadn't taken anything.

She noticed a green Camry parked out front in one of the few 15-minute parking spots, a man at the wheel. She'd had a Camry twenty years ago. She'd loved that car.

At four o'clock, the driver of a police van showed up with a two-wheeler, and in four trips hauled Brooke's boxes away. She went down the elevator with the driver to the street as the last ones were wheeled away, and was surprised by a wave of sadness.

As she turned, she noticed the green Camry still parked out front, a man still behind the wheel, surprised he hadn't been shooed away by security.

Chapter 3

Madeline woke up early the next morning, the luminous numbers of her clock reading 5:00, three hours before the alarm would go off. It was a Sunday after all, but she couldn't go back to sleep, not now. She worried about Coda Gems' future. They had to move, that was unavoidable, but they didn't have the money to stay in downtown Boston. So where could they go?

She threw off the down comforter and padded to the kitchen, put on a pot of coffee, and sat at the computer in her study scrolling through news updates but thinking about money until well after the sun rose.

She and Abby were in a real jam now, and there was no Brooke Sears to get them out of it.

***

When Cecil's doorbell rang at 7:15 a.m. on Monday he went downstairs. He knew who it was. Paige had sent him a text the night before saying that she'd stop by that morning. The woman was impervious to time zone changes. She should be dead asleep. Although just dead would be good.

Cecil opened the front door, Paige leaning against the railing in blue jeans and a motorcycle jacket, texting on her cell phone, her hair sticking up as if a bolt of lightning had struck her. And too much eye makeup, as usual. She looked up, went back to her text, and then shoved her cell in a jacket pocket.

She said, "Good to see you," and brushed past him into the living room. At the funeral reception she'd asked if she could borrow their mother's black

38

Mercedes, stored in his four-car garage, for a day or so. And he'd said yes. He needed to keep Paige friendly.

Paige said, "I'm sorry that I had to leave Mother's funeral lunch early, but like I said, I still get headaches. Bad ones."

Paige had been in a serious accident three months before on a movie set, knocked unconscious by an overhead jib, with a thirteen-inch gash on her thigh. Her injuries were serious enough that Brooke had flown out to Los Angeles.

Cecil followed Paige inside to the living room. "I did call Alfred about moving up the reading of Mother's will as soon as possible. He said tomorrow at two would be fine, and that his office would be in touch. I sent you a text."

"Alfred is an old gas bag. And yes, I got your text, and also yes, I did hear from his office too. But what did he say was in the will? Exactly?"

"Look, Paige, I got him to agree to move the meeting up by two weeks."

She slumped on the sofa and crossed her legs. "You didn't ask him? I thought you were going to find out exactly what was in it? I already know about her jewelry, but I need to know how much money Mother left me."

"You'll know tomorrow, for God's sake."

Paige repeated, "I told you I need to know. Now. It's important."

Typical Paige. She didn't say 'we' even though he was a beneficiary in Brooke's will too. She added, "I'm in an expensive business."

Paige must be in very big trouble if she couldn't even wait for a day. He handed her the keys to the Mercedes. "Relax, you'll know soon enough."

She sighed and sat up. "I should have gotten my share of Daddy's trust fund in one fell swoop when I turned twenty-one, instead of getting stuck with an annual dividend. That's how any normal rich, loving father would have set it up."

Cecil, tired of this old complaint, said, "Paige, who knows what Father was thinking? But three million dollars a year is a lot of money." He added, annoyed, "Why don't you try and live on that?"

Paige stood up and jammed the car keys in her pocket. "Spare me. I didn't come here for a lecture."

When Cecil was a teenager, his mother confided to him more than once that she was worried about Paige, and perhaps not having a father figure was the problem. That wasn't the problem. Paige had a mean, vicious streak and a taste for violence. It was a relief when she'd moved to Los Angeles for a career in film, bouncing around for years as a well-heeled assistant to a string of producers. And then after her divorce from one of them, Paige started her own production company, making slasher films or whatever they were called, where she could revel in blood for a living, even if it was fake blood. Which it was, as far as he knew.

"I can't believe the police are still keeping me out of Mother's place," Paige said. "I'd like to get in, check around. Take a look, you know? So when can we get in?"

Cecil said, noncommittally, "Soon, I should think."

He wasn't about to tell her they could get into their mother's townhouse at eight the next morning. He didn't want her poking around and getting in the way while he was there. She'd be curious about what he was looking for.

Instead he said, "Mother's car is parked in the garage. The clicker for the door is on the key ring. But can't you stay for a few minutes? We haven't talked, I mean really talked, since you've been back. Would you like a cup of tea?" He didn't want Paige to leave angry.

Paige looked at her watch. "Thanks, but no, I can't. I have a very important business call in half an hour."

"You said you're staying with friends?"

Paige nodded.

He knew her college friends, had known them for years. Two of them were in prison for assault and the odd drug charge. He was surprised they hadn't all been incarcerated by now.

He asked, "So when will you be heading back to Los Angeles?"

"I don't know. Why?"

He smiled, "Martha and I would like to have you over for dinner before you leave."

"I'll let you know. It depends. But do let me know if you talk to Alfred this afternoon or tonight, and ask him about Mother's will. Like I said, I need to know. It's very important." Paige stood up and Cecil walked her to the front door, where she kissed him on the cheek, and left.

He sighed.

***

That next afternoon, at 1:55, Madeline pushed through the heavy front door of the white-shoe law firm of Atkins & Rogers in Wellesley, an upscale Boston suburb. The reception area whispered Old Money with Persian rugs and black lacquer furniture. And what could well be a real Renoir on the wall. Good thing she was in cashmere.

On Saturday morning, Alfred Atkins's assistant, Meghan, a woman with a no-nonsense voice, had summoned her to the meeting, apologizing for the short notice. She told Madeline it involved issues concerning Brooke Sears's estate, gave her the address of their law office, and with a swift goodbye, disconnected.

Madeline hung up and stared at the phone. Why had she been summoned? Probably Brooke wanted her to do something. Madeline wouldn't put it past Brooke to be giving her instructions from the grave. Madeline sighed. Still, a part of her would miss Brooke. A small part.

In the reception area Madeline sat in one of the black lacquer chairs when, at exactly two, Meghan, a tall woman in her late twenties with a mane of tawny blonde hair led her to a small conference room. Cecil and Paige sat at one end of the table talking in whispers, and looked up in surprise when Madeline walked in. Paige was dressed in black, with a big black tattoo on her right forearm of the word 'Daddy' in bold, gothic lettering. Definitely a statement there. The handsome Cecil was in a dark blue suit, designer again, and a stark-white shirt. He pulled a pen out of his pocket and toyed with it, watching Madeline. Curious.

A huge window ran the length of the room behind them, overlooking a pale pond with a flock of arrogant swans.

At that moment a tall, thin man in his sixties wearing a pale gray suit and a face to match came in through a side door and stared at Madeline over his rimless glasses as he walked up to the conference table. "I'm Alfred Atkins, the estate attorney and trustee for the Sears's family. Thank you for coming."

She recognized him from Brooke's funeral. It was the glasses. Brooke had mentioned Alfred to Madeline a couple of times, although she always called him 'Dear Alfred.' Madeline had no idea what he did for Brooke, until now. He started to introduce her to Cecil and Paige, but she interrupted. "Thank you, but we've already met," and walked over to shake hands. Madeline was careful not to stare at Paige's tattoo.

Madeline sat in the empty chair next to Cecil, who whispered, "Not to be rude, but why are you here?"

Well, that was rude, so she whispered back, "Why do you think? Your mother wanted me here." And she looked away.

Alfred took a seat at the head of the table, opened a thick file folder and looked at Cecil, who nodded. Alfred cleared his throat, and all eyes were on him. The room was so quiet one could hear a feather drop.

"Thank you all for coming," said Alfred. He nodded to Cecil and Paige. "I have copies of your mother's trust instrument for both of you. As Brooke has already told you, she felt no need to provide either of you with additional financial support because you are both beneficiaries of your father's trust fund, and years down the road of course, the deceased sibling's distributions will automatically revert to the survivor. Nonetheless, she has included both of you in her will." He adjusted his glasses. "The legal term is a pour-over will, so there will be no need for probate. The specific bequests will be distributed as soon as possible."

Madeline watched Paige turn and smile at Cecil.

Alfred cleared his throat and continued, "Again, as you know, Brooke placed the bulk of her estate, including her investments, and her townhouse in a trust benefitting the Museum of Fine Arts." He glanced down at the papers in a thick file. "For Paige," and he nodded to her, Paige's eyes glued on him as he continued, "she has left her diamond engagement and wedding rings. Which were unfortunately stolen the night of her death. However, they were insured, so if they are not recovered within the next year a claim will be filed on your behalf." A pause. "In addition, your mother also left you all of her clothing. And the sum of fifty thousand dollars."

42

Alfred turned to Cecil. "And to you, she left her automobile, a Mercedes Benz, along with the books in her library that include," he looked down at papers in his folder, "fifteen first editions, and a similar sum of fifty thousand dollars." He stopped and in the silence flipped to another page in the file.

Paige said, her voice sharp, "That's it? There's more, isn't there?"

Alfred sighed. "Yes, there is." He glanced at Paige, then Cecil, with no expression on his face. "Your mother made an amendment to her will a couple of months ago, which was notarized here in this office. I have a copy for each of you. And one for Madeline."

Alfred turned to Madeline, who leaned forward, surprised.

The lawyer said, "I am now reading directly from Brooke's amendment." He glanced around the dead-silent room and continued, "I leave my entire gem collection, consisting of twenty-five pieces of pearl and diamond jewelry, and one Cartier watch," another pause as Alfred cleared his throat, "to my dear friend, Madeline Lane, as a thank you for being a true-blue friend."

A silence fell in the room, and Paige's eyes whirled from Alfred to Cecil and back to Alfred.

Paige said, "What? What did you say?"

Alfred repeated the wording in the amendment, the eyes of the three at the conference table glued to their copies. Alfred handed another page to Madeline, Cecil and Paige. "This is a list of the pieces of jewelry that Brooke left to Madeline."

Alfred closed the folder and continued, looking at Madeline again, who sat in shocked silence, "Do note that two pearl and diamond bracelets on that list were also apparently stolen at the time of Brooke's death. Should those pieces be recovered, they will be transferred to you. And if they are not recovered within a year an insurance claim on your behalf as well. And so…"

"Stop right now," shouted Paige, as she shot out of her chair, the palms of her hands flat on the conference table. She leaned toward Alfred, her voice shaking. "You can't be serious. My mother's jewelry going to…to this Madeline woman?" Paige didn't look at Madeline but continued, "This can't be right! There's been a mistake. This is all wrong. I was to get her jewelry.

She told me that years ago. That's what she said!"

Astonished, Madeline could only stare at Alfred, her heart pounding. What? Brooke had left her entire jewelry collection to her? To her? All of it, except her wedding rings? She looked at Cecil and back again to Alfred, both of them now staring at Paige.

Madeline glanced down at the sheet in front of her. The most valuable was a Cartier Art Deco necklace, three strands of nine-millimeter pearls, with an eleven-carat diamond pendant. The necklace alone had to be worth well over one hundred and fifty thousand dollars. And now all of Brooke's jewelry was hers? She knew every piece on the list, all of them pearl, and all but one by Cartier or Tiffany.

"And so outside of small settlements for two household staff members, that covers Mrs. Sear's specific bequests," Alfred said.

Still standing, Paige's face now dead white, she said, her voice shrill, "This can't be true! I can't believe it! There's been a mistake! A very big mistake. She jerked her head toward Madeline.

Alfred said, "There is no mistake. This constitutes your mother's final wishes regarding the disposition of her jewelry."

Furious, Paige strode around the table and up to Alfred. With a nasty smile she said, "This is just too much. I mean really. I don't believe you. Let me see the original of that amendment, or whatever you call it. My mother told me years ago she was leaving all of her jewelry to me. To me. That's what she said, that she was leaving all of it to me!"

Paige grabbed the paper out of his hand, all eyes in the room on her as she scanned the page, and signature lines, and notary seal. When she glanced up, Madeline looked away. After a long, tense moment Paige threw it on the conference table and said to Alfred, "I can't believe this. I'll get a lawyer. I'll contest this and…"

Alfred stopped her, saying to Cecil and Paige, "I suggest we go over all of this in my office. Plus, I will need bank instructions from you regarding wiring of the funds. I'll also review the terms of the trust for the museum, and the process for them to take possession of her townhouse. And…"

Paige interrupted, shouting again, "So all I get is a lousy fifty grand and her designer clothes? Like I'd ever wear any of them. Ever." Her voice mocking now. "Oh, I almost forgot, there's the insurance money for her wedding rings, which god knows how long that will take before I see any of it. I'll be lucky to get thirty thousand, if that."

Alfred said, "I am sorry, Paige. Brooke told me she'd discussed the terms of her will with you and your brother when she set it up twenty ago, and yes, she had left all of her jewelry to you at that time. However, she changed the jewelry clause…" he looked down at the amendment, "two and a half months ago. I apologize for the surprise. I was not aware she hadn't told you about this change and—"

Cecil interrupted, "Mother did tell us about the terms, in general, some time ago, although she wasn't specific about the amount of cash. And she did say Paige was to receive her entire jewelry collection, which no longer appears to be the case. I'm sure you can appreciate this is an unpleasant surprise for my sister. Neither of us knew anything about this amendment."

Alfred nodded. "Well, as I said, Brooke recently asked me to draft it." He nodded to the original document on the conference table. "And it does reflect her wishes. As trustee, I've already sealed her safe deposit box which contains her jewelry, and I will oversee the transfer of the jewelry to Ms. Lane at her convenience."

He turned to Paige. "And I'll set up a time for you to collect the clothing from Brooke's townhouse." And then to Cecil, "I'll also let you know when you can have the books in her library picked up. I understand her Mercedes is already in your possession?"

Cecil nodded. "Yes, I've been storing it for her. However, I recently lent the Mercedes to Paige."

Alfred said, "Well, I suggest you take it back until I can finalize the transfer of the title."

Paige snapped, "Who cares about the damn car?" She whirled to face Madeline, her voice shaking. "I can't believe this is happening. Mother meant to leave her pearl jewelry to me." Madeline could only look at her, wide-eyed as Paige continued, "That's what she told me. That's what she said. Including the pearl necklace with the huge diamond that my father gave her

45

as a wedding present. All of it was to go to me. To stay in the family. In the family," she repeated. "It was to have been mine. Not yours. I'd like to know how you got her to change her mind, that's what I'd like to know."

Paige turned again to Alfred, clipping her words. "And to be honest, when Mother said she'd leave my brother and me each a small sum I didn't realize it would be so...so tiny."

Alfred said, "I'm sorry you're disappointed, Paige. Please sit down. As I suggested, we can review your mother's trust documents along with the amendment in my office now if you'd like." He looked at Madeline and said, "There is no need for you to stay, Ms. Lane. I will be in touch shortly regarding the transfer of Brooke's jewelry."

Madeline stood up from the conference table. Since this didn't seem to be a good time for handshakes, she nodded to a furious Paige and a stone-faced Cecil and headed to the door. As she left she heard Cecil say, "Alfred, I'll be right back. I want to have a word with Madeline."

Madeline didn't stop, and let the door swing shut behind her.

***

Cecil caught up to Madeline in the reception area. "Do you have a minute?"

She nodded and they walked out the front door together. At this point Cecil was about the last person on earth she wanted to talk to, Paige being dead last.

Madeline began, "Cecil, this is such a...surprise. Just so you know, I had no idea your mother would leave me her pearls. She never said a word. Nothing." Madeline thought for a second about apologizing. For what? So she didn't.

"Mother did have a mind of her own."

Madeline headed to her car, Cecil walking beside her, the only sound the click of her high heels on the pavement.

"I just want to double-check that the boxes at your place contained *all* of Mother's papers. Nothing left behind? Accidentally? Like a manila envelope?" Cecil said.

46

The man was really too much.

Madeline didn't look at him as she replied, "I am sorry, Cecil, but nothing was left out. Nothing." She stopped beside her car and pulled out the keys

Cecil ran his fingers through his long black hair. "But, Madeline, I..." he began, his voice rising, then started over, his voice calmer. "I was at Mother's townhouse this morning and I thought for sure the manila envelope would be in her study somewhere. I went through everything, but couldn't find it. It should have been, but it wasn't. And I spent two hours looking for it in her library." He looked at his watch. "Anyway, it seems to be missing."

"Missing? That's too bad. I'm sorry to hear that."

"Yes, it's an old envelope, with the initials AP, quite large on the front. Inside were loose pages of family historical and financial records, held together with a big black clip. Which belong to the Sears family. Anyway, I have to fly down to Washington in an hour...I saw it there, on her desk that last morning, the day she...but now it's gone."

"Unfortunately, Cecil, I can't help you. I never saw anything like that."

Cecil dropped the smile. "You didn't? I thought maybe she may have given it to you for safekeeping and—"

Madeline shook her head. "Safekeeping? No, Cecil, she did not."

"By the way, did you happen to go through any of her boxes? You must have been a little bit curious after they were delivered. Anyone would have been."

She stared him in the eye and muttered, "No, I didn't go through them. I'm not the curious type."

Although to be honest she had opened one carton and flipped through the folders for about a minute. Alright five minutes. But now was not the time to admit that to Cecil.

Cecil continued, "You're absolutely positive you never saw a manila envelope? About ten by twelve? Quite thick?"

"I'm positive. Look, Brooke never said anything to me about an envelope. Just that she wanted me to go through her boxes with her. That was it."

Cecil took a step towards her, his eyes a hard, slate gray now. A muscle in his jaw twitched. "I need to find that envelope. Did you perhaps take it by mistake?"

"Cecil, are you hard of hearing? How many times do I have to tell you I have no idea what your mother did with this envelope? I don't know where it is. Never heard it mentioned, never saw it, never touched it. Maybe it's in her library, stuck between the books or something. There must be at least a thousand books in there."

He stared at her, his face blank. A vein pulsed in his temple. She continued in a conciliatory tone. "You know what, maybe the police took it when they were collecting evidence from the scene."

Cecil shook his head. "No, the police don't have it. I went through their evidence list, and a manila envelope, or any kind of envelope wasn't on it. I specifically asked, and they said no." He stood waiting, watching her.

Madeline had learned over the years that the rich could obsess over the oddest things. Which was tedious. Like now. She jangled her car keys, wanting this uncomfortable conversation to be over. "Well, I am sorry that I can't help you. I hope you find this envelope. And, Cecil, like I told you, I had no idea that Brooke would leave me her jewelry. None."

"Yes, well Paige is not handling the loss of Mother's pearls very well." He glanced back at the law office. "I should get back and talk to Alfred and..." He stopped in mid-sentence then added, "but maybe my mother left it in your store that last morning when she came to see you. I saw her later that day and she said she'd been to your shop, or whatever you call it. It could be there. I would appreciate it if you could check? And call me?"

Madeline shook her head. "I'm positive she didn't leave anything behind. Brooke was there for less than fifteen minutes and didn't leave anything on my desk or on the chair. Or anywhere in the store. I'm sorry, but I can't help you."

Cecil turned and headed back to the lawyer's office.

Madeline called after him. "Cecil, about your mother's boxes. Would it be helpful if I went through them with you? Once you get them back from the police? We could go through them together, before you turn them over to the Boston Public Library. I'll have a good sense as to what she might not want to have included. Your mother would want me to do that."

His face was pale now and his words clipped. "You know what, thanks but no thanks, Madeline. The Sears family doesn't need, much less want any of your assistance. You somehow convinced my mother to turn against Paige, for God's sake. So no, I don't want you poking around in our family business any longer. At all. Is that clear? You got what you wanted, so stay away from the Sears family. Just keep away."

Madeline felt her face flush red as if he'd slapped her.

Cecil stalked back to the building, yanked open the front door and disappeared inside.

Madeline stared after him. This was not how she wanted her relationship with Brooke's children to end. Both of them now hated her, although she didn't care much for either of them either, especially Paige.

Madeline clicked open her car. Well, that was an ugly scene. Nothing to be done about it though. She'd just have to make sure to steer clear of the Sears family. Which wouldn't be all that hard since she had no reason to see or speak to either of them ever again.

***

Madeline sped out of the parking lot, tires squealing, but once she was on the expressway she calmed down. After all, she was now, for all intents and purposes, a mini-heiress, the sole owner of Brooke Sears' collection of pearl jewelry.

But as she wove through traffic on her way back to Downtown Crossing, all she felt was guilt. She tried to remember the exact words Brooke had written in the trust document, but the only phrase that stuck in her mind was "True-Blue Friend."

So that was how Brooke thought of her? As a true-blue friend? Which wasn't how she thought of herself at all. Because she hadn't been. Not really. She hadn't been a friend to Brooke, not in the real sense of the word.

As Madeline parked her car in the garage a block from Coda Gems she thought about Abby. Abby would be thrilled at her news, and she brightened at the thought. Yes, Coda Gems would be just fine now. Their worries were over.

***

Madeline took the elevator up seven floors and rushed down the hall to Coda Gems, all but bumping into two customers on their way out.

Abby, on her cell phone, was standing by the front glass case, and looked up when she walked in. Madeline mouthed to Abby, "Hang up. Now."

So Abby said into the phone, "Something has come up. I have to go, but I'll call back later." She dropped her phone into her pocket.

In a rush of words, Madeline told her about the meeting in the lawyer's office, and ended with, "So Brooke left me her whole collection of jewelry. I'm not sure yet what it's worth, could be as much as seven hundred and fifty thousand dollars. Maybe even more! She left me all of her jewelry, except for her diamond wedding rings. She willed those to her daughter, Paige."

"What? This is a joke, right? You can't be serious. Brooke left all of her jewelry to you?" Abby said.

"Yes, she did. She absolutely did. The lawyer said Brooke changed her will a couple of months ago, adding me as a beneficiary."

"Today, you learned this just today at the meeting with the lawyer in Wellesley? You told me you thought you were called to the lawyer's office because Brooke probably wanted you to do something and you were…not happy about it."

"Well, I was wrong," Madeline said. "Very, very wrong. So anyway, this means we're rich. Well, a bit rich. So pack up your calculator and your computer. We can move to Newbury Street now."

"What?"

Madeline laughed. "Yes, to the expensive end of Newbury Street, of course. Nothing but the best for Coda Gems."

"Well, a nice thought, but that seems a bit rash."

"Not to me."

Abby blinked a couple of times. "But…what did Brooke's children say? About her pearls?"

Madeline dropped the smile. "They were stunned. Paige especially. Actually, she was livid. Spitting mad."

"Well, whatever," Abby said. "Still, I wouldn't have thought Brooke capable of such an amazing gesture. No, wait, it's not amazing, it's unbelievable. But why? Why would she do that?"

Madeline sighed. "To be honest, I have no idea. What I do know is that I am very, very lucky. And after her lawyer hands over her pearls, we'll sell several of the pieces right away." She added with a broad smile, "Which means we can start looking at a new space on Newbury Street. Like tomorrow."

"Madeline, that is wonderful news for you, but I can't afford to—"

"Abby, we're partners, and since Coda Gems has to move, it should be to a great place. Not just good, or God forbid average, but great. And Brooke's pearls can make great happen. I'll take care of the rent for the first year or so until we're established in our new location. And after that, we'll split the rent again."

"But Madeline, I can't—"

"Of course you can. We're in this together. After all, when we opened Coda Gems and had no...well, very little money, you spotted me. So it's my turn now. I just got a lucky break, because if Brooke hadn't..." her voice trailed off.

"We'll talk about the rent part later." Abby shook her head. "So our best customer is murdered and leaves you a fortune in pearls. Just in the nick of time? Sounds like a soap opera."

Madeline said, "You're right, it is a soap opera." She glanced around their small space, including the view from their forlorn window. "I don't want to stay here one day longer than necessary. We'll find a space, a street-level space on Newbury Street, and we'll have the crème de la crème lining up."

"Just checking, but you have all this in writing?"

"Absolutely. So we can move to a *very* good new location now." Madeline reached into her purse and handed her Brooke's amendment and the list of her jewelry.

Abby read it once, then twice, and with tears glinting in her eyes gave Madeline a bear hug. "But we do need to look at spaces that have reasonable rents. We shouldn't get carried away."

Madeline stepped back. "Getting carried away won't hurt."

Abby looked at her. "There is a difference between getting carried away and leaping off a precipice. We have to be reasonable."

"I hate reasonable, it's so boring. How about we get reasonably carried away? We can talk about it over dinner tonight at Mistral." She pulled out her cell phone. "I'll make a reservation now."

Upscale and French, the restaurant in the South End was one of Boston's most expensive. Madeline had never been there, and she guessed Abby hadn't either. Great news demanded a classy celebration.

***

Three hours later at Mistral, the partners had finished their appetizers, Portobello mushrooms and steamed mussels, and one bottle of Dom Pérignon, with a second on ice by their table. As their entrees were set in front of them, Abby, who rarely drank, signaled to the waiter to open the second bottle, and Madeline gave her a minute by minute account of the scene in the lawyer's office, including Paige's theatrics.

Abby said, "I'm not surprised Brooke's daughter was upset."

The waiter uncorked the bottle of champagne. Even the pop sounded expensive.

As he poured champagne into Madeline's glass, she said to Abby, "Paige even called me 'that woman.'"

"Will she contest it?"

"She could, I suppose, but she'd have to have grounds. Besides, Paige is already rich. She's been rich all of her life." Madeline shrugged. "She'll be fine. She'll get over it. She'll have to."

Abby looked at her and lifted up her champagne glass. "I hope so. Anyway, here's to the wonderful Brooke Sears who has saved Coda Gems. Again. May she rest in peace."

They clinked glasses and Madeline's eyes filled with tears, but not from grief. From regret. Because there was no way she could ever thank Brooke.

No way to show her gratitude. She downed her glass of champagne.

Chapter 4

Later, at home, Madeline couldn't sleep, but this time not from worry. Instead, in her mind she kept going over the meeting at the lawyer's office that afternoon as if it were a scene in a movie. There were the two smug and entitled heirs, the aged lawyer, the heroine (that would be her), and the room, hushed and all tense. Then the bombshell.

At two a.m., Madeline gave up on sleep. At the desk in her study, she pulled out the list of Brooke's pearls. What had she done to deserve this extraordinary gift? Brooke had called her a true-blue friend, but she hadn't been all that much of a friend. Not really.

Madeline thought about Brooke's boxes, and wished she'd never told Detective Amick she had them. After all, wasn't possession nine-tenths of the law? And she wished again she hadn't gone to the police station the morning after Brooke's murder.

Unfortunately, it was too late to do anything about Brooke's papers.

Except she still could be a true-blue friend. It wasn't too late. She could at least try to stop Cecil from turning over Brooke's manila envelope of papers that he was so anxious to find. Yes, that was something she could do for Brooke. She could at the very least make an effort. She could at least try.

On the other hand, maybe the thieves had taken Brooke's papers that night? But why would they bother to grab an old envelope which might or might not have been on Brooke's desk? The thieves would have been after jewels or money. Something valuable they could sell right away.

Since it was a stretch that the thieves would have grabbed a manila envelope, it was most likely in Brooke's townhouse, somewhere, so Cecil would be sure to find it. Of course he'd find it. Cecil was the tenacious type.

Which meant she needed to find the damn envelope first, before the obnoxious Cecil got his hands on it.

Otherwise, she'd be dogged by guilt for the rest of her life.

After all, she did know how to get into Brooke's townhouse. So she'd go there and look for the damn envelope. Maybe find it, maybe not. But at least she'd have done *something* for Brooke.

The more she thought about it, the more Madeline knew she had to do it. She owed that to Brooke. She wouldn't spend a lot of time in the townhouse, half an hour or so would be good. And then Madeline would actually be a real true-blue friend.

And besides, it wasn't like she'd be committing a felony, exactly.

***

When Madeline walked into the store the next morning, she had the whole caper—such a good word, with its hint of danger and derring-do—figured out. But she had to do it that night before she lost her nerve. And before the Museum of Fine Arts changed the locks. But what if they'd changed them already? Maybe they had. But probably not. Nonprofits weren't all that quick about getting anything done.

Six months earlier, Brooke had called her from Palm Beach and told her to pick up a pair of gray shoes from her closet and FedEx them to her. She gave Madeline specific instructions on how to get inside, and how to disarm her security system.

So it should be easy to get into Brooke's place again. That is, if no one was in the townhouse, and if the key was still taped under the lip of the boxwood planter on her back deck. And if the security password hadn't been changed. A lot of ifs. The only good part was that Cecil said he had to be in Washington.

Madeline knew better than to mention her idea to Abby, who would've had a heart attack. And would definitely try to stop her. So she told Abby that she had forgotten about a doctor's appointment, and left the store at four.

As Madeline walked out of the store, she felt almost noble about her grand plan of breaking into Brooke's place. Especially since she believed she could get away with it.

***

But once she was back home, Madeline changed her mind twice about breaking into Brooke's. The whole idea was ridiculous. Crazy. What if the police showed up? How would she explain herself to the prickly Detective Amick? No, the whole idea was stupid. And risky.

But one thing she did know for sure, it was tonight, or never. It was the never part that got to her. She changed into a pair of black sweat pants and sweater and stuffed her blonde hair under a black beret, and grabbed a pair of driving gloves.

A flashlight. She'd almost forgotten to bring a flashlight, then grabbed one from a drawer in the kitchen. If she'd had a gun she would have grabbed that too. But she didn't own a gun. In fact she'd fired a gun exactly six times in her life, hunting wild turkeys in a field one day years ago with friends in Concord. She didn't have the heart to aim at one of those big beautiful birds, so she shot at a couple of stop signs instead. And missed every time. She really should take a gun class sometime, you never knew, it could be helpful. Annie Oakley had been a hell of a shot.

She went out the door, took the elevator down to the garage, and eased her car into rush hour traffic, dusk just setting in, and drove toward Louisburg Square, the road a crush of cars. She noticed the drivers all looked menacing in the dim light. Were they staring at her? She made two illegal left-hand turns and drove the wrong way down an alley, checking her rear view mirror every few seconds. No one seemed to be following her.

She just wanted to get this night over with, and prove to herself that she was indeed a true-blue friend to Brooke.

***

Fifteen minutes later Madeline parked two blocks from Brooke's townhouse, walked all the way around it, making sure no lights were on, then slipped around the back and hurried up the steps to the teak deck. Good, the big boxwood planter was still there. Was the key still taped under the inside rim? In the dark, Madeline moved her fingers lightly along the inside of the rim, her eyes watching for any movement in the dark alley. The key had to be there. But halfway around she'd felt nothing. And froze. What if this was how the burglar had gained entry the night Brooke was murdered? But how could they know? She shuddered and continued feeling her way around the rim. It just wasn't there.

And then her fingers felt a long bump. And tape. The key. She took off her gloves, and pried off the tape with her fingernails. Breaking one. Not taking her eyes off the alley.

The key to Brooke's back door dropped into her palm.

So far so good. She glanced around in all directions, no one walking down the alley to see her. Someone could be watching from a dark window, but she'd have to take that risk. She swallowed hard and slid the key in the lock, ready to run off in case an alarm she didn't know about blared away. But there was nothing, only silence. The key turned effortlessly and she opened Brooke's back door.

She stepped inside and saw the blinking red lights on the security panel. No problem, since Brooke had told her about the two systems. Madeline typed in Brooke's password, Franklin1, and the red light for the security cameras went dark, and then with the password Eleanor1 the flashing light for all of the door and window alarms also shut off. Madeline turned on her flashlight, and moved down the hallway.

Madeline didn't bother with Brooke's study, since Cecil had said he'd already searched that room. She hurried into the living room, with its two long sofas, a couple of cabinets and end tables, and a big screen TV. She jerked out the drawers of the Chippendale cabinets and end tables. Nothing except TV remotes and stacks of magazines and stationery. Just in case, she tossed the sofa pillows and looked under the cushions and then under the sofa. More nothing.

What about the library? Wasn't that the favorite room for secrets, with sliding panels and hollowed-out books? Cecil said he'd already checked there, but she had to at least take a look. She rushed up to the second-floor library, and turned on the flashlight for a quick second. The room looked like it had been hit by a tornado, hundreds of books tossed in piles in the middle of the room, half the shelves empty. So maybe Cecil had already found the damn envelope, but maybe not. She didn't have time to sort through the piles or the books still on the shelves, so Madeline slipped out of the library and searched through the two guest bedrooms on the second floor, sifting through drawer after drawer of clothes and bedding, flicking on her flashlight every minute or two. The good part was she wasn't looking for something small. A ten-by-twelve-inch envelope was hardly small. She even looked under the corners of the mattresses in each bedroom. The two bathrooms took less than ten minutes. She combed through the stacks of towels and sheets and pillowcases, and then through drawers of Pecksniff's soap, shampoos and conditioners.

Madeline checked her watch. She'd been at Brooke's for almost an hour already. But she wasn't about to leave. Not yet.

There was nothing in the master bedroom except drawers of sweaters and pullovers, and lingerie, and two large closets of designer dresses, slacks and shoe racks. This was taking forever.

She flew downstairs, by this time her heart in a constant state of thud. In the dining room, with wide windows facing the garden, was an antique Chinese table and chairs, five tall hand-painted chinoiserie screens, and a wide sideboard cabinet. She opened all the doors and drawers, but saw only shelves of plates that she pushed aside, rows of coffee cups hanging on hooks, and two drawers of placemats and napkins.

That only left the kitchen. Brooke told her she once had a cook come in four days a week, but she let him go a year ago, and just had take-out delivered, or went to restaurants in Beacon Hill with friends for dinner. Which meant she rarely cooked.

Madeline heard a car pull up down the street and rushed to the window. Just a taxi, but she waited until a man got out of the cab and went up the front steps of a townhouse across the street. Madeline checked her watch. She'd look for ten more minutes and then she absolutely had to leave.

***

Madeline hurried down the hall into the kitchen, its floor to ceiling windows overlooking the street, a pale-yellow light from the rising moon filling a room of stainless-steel Wolf appliances, and wide stretches of olive-green granite counters. She yanked open drawers of flatware and linen napkins, and cabinets full of dishes and stemware, and then shelves of spices and condiments and cans of soup. Soup? Madeline was pretty much done with this last room, and anxious to leave. The last long cabinet held only pots and pans hanging from thick, sturdy hooks. Nothing. She yanked open the door of a cabinet under the counter, just two shelves of celebrity chef cookbooks, and almost shut the door. But changed her mind. She got on her hands and knees and flipped through the rows of heavy books.

And there, way in the back, stuck behind a row of Julia Child cookbooks, was something tall and yellow. A manila envelope? She flicked on her flashlight for a second. Yes, an old, wrinkled, manila envelope.

Just as she reached for it, she heard the back door open and close, then the click of a light switch. Thirty long seconds later she heard a dull whirring sound and looked up. A camera in the corner was moving. So whoever entered had turned on the security cameras. She had to get out of Brooke's townhouse, now. Before they activated the door alarms.

***

Madeline grabbed the envelope, and in the dim light, her heart in her throat, she slid out of the kitchen and down the long hall to the front door and opened it, ready to sprint if the door alarm went off.

It didn't.

Madeline slipped outside, easing the door shut behind her, and walked, as normally as possible, across the street. In the shadows of the trees, she looked back at the townhouse, and saw the lights go on in the library on the second floor. Cecil was in one of the library windows staring down at the street below. Could he see her? She didn't think so but she backed further into the shadows, not breathing. So he was back from Washington. What was he doing here? Looking for the envelope?

Staying in the shadows she walked back to her car, the envelope tight under her right arm, glancing back over her shoulder only at cross streets.

The neighbors she passed on the sidewalk paid no attention to her, and the few passing cars did not slow.

***

When Madeline got close to her car, she clicked it open and slid in, tossed the envelope on the passenger seat, and started the engine. Her hands were shaking, her eyes flicking between the rear-view mirror and the side one as she pulled out onto the street. There were two cars behind her, but they turned off after a couple of blocks.

Madeline hit the accelerator, took a right turn, and sped off into the darkness toward home.

At a long red light at Boylston Street, Madeline heaved a sigh of relief that she hadn't gotten caught. She turned on an overhead light and glanced at the old envelope on the seat beside her, the letters AP in big black magic marker scrawled on the front. She'd found it, and had beaten Cecil to it! Whatever it was.

But now that she had the damn envelope, what should she do? She smiled. That didn't matter. Even if the envelope was full of old, faded estate receipts, this had been worth the risk. She had it, and Cecil didn't, and she'd make sure it stayed that way. The important point was that she'd honored her obligation to Brooke. She felt very true-blue. And as a double bonus, she'd just made Cecil's life miserable.

***

Madeline walked through her front door, turned on all the lights, and dropped her keys on the hall table. She set the manila envelope on the blue granite countertop in her kitchen. She'd done it. She'd actually pulled it off! Still nervous, she went back and threw the dead bolt on her front door as an extra precaution. Just in case someone had followed her, although she was probably just being paranoid. Nevertheless, she walked back to the kitchen island, and pulled down the shades before she picked up the envelope. In the light she could see it was stiff with age. She pried open the clasp, one of the old prongs snapping off. She gently opened the flap, and inside a thick stack of pages were held together by a wide, old-fashioned clip. Just like Cecil had described.

Except the clip wasn't holding together old financial records, but an old, tattered manuscript. She stared at the faded cover page, the title and the author's name. Holding her breath, Madeline went back to her front door and double-checked then triple-checked the lock.

The cover page read *Answered Prayers* and underneath that, *By Truman Capote*.

ACT II

Chapter 5

Madeline couldn't take her eyes off the title page. This had to be a joke, this could not possibly be, this just could not be the most famously lost manuscript of the twentieth century. She flipped through the typed pages of *Answered Prayers*. She held a page close to her nose; it smelled musty. Whatever, this couldn't be Capote's last work. That was just not possible. The beat-up manuscript was likely just an old prank.

In Capote's many interviews after *In Cold Blood*, his true-crime best-seller that created a sensation, Capote said his next book, *Answered Prayers*, would also be based on real life. "It will be a contemporary equivalent to Proust's masterpiece," he'd told reporters. "Everything in my next book will be true, all of it true. It will *not* be a work of fiction."

That part was true. But what Capote didn't mention was that in his new book he would turn his basilisk eyes on the small world of the very rich, part-aristocratic, part-café society of Manhattan, a world that included his best and dearest friends.

And he would betray them all by spilling their deepest secrets.

To whet the public's appetite, in 1975 Capote gave *Esquire* permission to publish the first three chapters of his still-in-progress book. An 'installment' he called these chapters that followed through on his 'real life' statement, because the barely disguised main characters were all real, all famous, all rich. And powerful. And Capote's deadly pen exposed their dysfunctional lives and their closeted secrets, from infidelity to sexual orientation to murder.

But when the issues of *Esquire* hit the newsstands in the relatively conservative 1970's, it was tantamount to Capote's social suicide, and he was dropped by his high-profile New York friends. The hard-thud kind. The weekends with William and Babe Paley were over, the chatty phone calls and lunches with Slim Keith and CZ Guest and his "Swans" a thing of the past. All gone. His New York friends closed ranks and shut Truman out of their lives.

He complained to anyone who would listen. "I'm a writer, for God's sake. I write what I know." He didn't add that he was also a writer looking for revenge.

So Capote soldiered on, basically alone over the next years, working on *Answered Prayers* between bouts of rehab for alcohol and drug addiction, until he died in 1984 of liver cancer and alcohol poisoning. His death was not a shock since he'd been publicly tottering toward it for years. The shock was that his much-touted manuscript was nowhere to be found. Anywhere. The battered pages he'd carried around with him for years, reading parts to anyone who would listen, had disappeared.

That night Madeline took the manuscript into the living room and curled up on the black leather sofa by the fireplace. And yes, this old manuscript began with the three chapters published years ago in *Esquire*, which she had read a long time ago, but hadn't given them much thought. But she did now. No wonder Babe Paley, wife of CBS founder and chairman William Paley, never spoke to Truman again. And then Madeline read the seven chapters that followed, stories that had never been published, the last one with the spine-rattling title "Father Flanagan's All-Night Nigger Queen Kosher Café."

Capote had said that he was constructing his new book like a gun. "There's the handle, the trigger, the barrel, and finally the bullet."

Some bullet.

In his book Capote had turned against the rich and famous women he called his dearest friends. But despite their years of long, breathless phone calls and whispered confidences, he'd come to believe these women thought of him as a joke, nothing more than an interesting, and very entertaining joke. An odd little gay man with a high-pitched voice they kept around to amuse themselves. So in *Answered Prayers*, the book he knew would be his last, Capote turned on them, striking back with the ultimate weapon. Their secrets.

After Capote died, his literary agent, along with his long-time lover, and a team of lawyers searched for the manuscript of *Answered Prayers* at his condo in the United Nations Towers, and his beach house at Sagaponack in the Hamptons. But his salacious manuscript was not in either of his homes. Random House was an interested party in the search as well, since they had already given him a significant advance, and had a signed million-dollar contract for his new book.

But they all came up empty-handed. Capote's manuscript was never found, even though the literary world teemed with theories about it. Some were positive the manuscript was in a safe-deposit box in a bank. Somewhere. Others that he had stashed it in a locker at a Greyhound bus depot in Los Angeles.

However, as the years passed with the manuscript still missing, a new theory surfaced, that the completed manuscript never existed. That Capote had written the first three chapters, and that was it. Even though he had carried a tattered manuscript with him everywhere for eight years after, and talked incessantly about his *Answered Prayers* work in progress, that's all it had been, just talk.

Madeline picked up the manuscript. So were all the theories wrong?

She went back to the beginning and read the entire crinkled manuscript, the stories narrated by Capote's fictional character P.B. Jones, a writer who churned out a journal of his friendships with the rich and entitled.Sleeping with many, gossiping about all, his stories ranging from the knife-edge pornographic to hard-core gossip, to a story of a prosaic cruise along the Turkish coast. All about real, living and rich people, thinly disguised.

But Capote's next to last chapter, "A Brahmin Slut" was a shock, the hair standing up on the back of Madeline's neck as she read it. And then she read it again. And again. Because there was no doubt, the main character in that story was Brooke Sears.

Yes, the young woman was definitely a young Brooke, a Boston blue-blood with jet-black hair and pale gray eyes. A woman who loved pearls, and had a custom-made collar for her white borzoi hound studded with them. A wild child who loved martinis and jazz and partied through the night. But the wild child ended up marrying a bookish, East Coast Standard Oil heir. Yes, it was Brooke all right. And in the story, both families were glad the beautiful rebel had settled down to a dull, patrician life.

Except according to Capote, she hadn't.

At her husband's estate in Bar Harbor as well as at his Manhattan townhouse the woman conducted a long and fiery doomed affair with the son of a Mafia crime boss, a twenty-seven-year-old man named Benedict, who ran a drug syndicate for the family. A man with long, dark, swept-back hair, and a sensuous face of drowsy lips and black-lashed eyes. A handsome, dangerous man, like Lord Byron.

And a man who got the married woman pregnant.

But the woman had a mind of her own and kept the child, and her rich, Brahmin husband never suspected the baby was not his. Scandal avoided. A child that the narrator called "The First Born." And the affair continued, with Capote even detailing their sexual positions in his story, his descriptions blunt, explicit.

In the story the unsuspecting husband even set up the child that was not his with a $200-million-dollar-trust fund. And then a tragedy. The sensual Benedict was murdered by Kane, a member of his crime family, and the heartbroken woman went back to her blue-blood life, keeping the memory of her dead lover locked in her heart.

Madeline read the chapter at least five more times, parsing over every word. There was no doubt the woman in the story was Brooke. But was it true? There could well have been an affair, but an illegitimate child? Regardless, if this was Capote's manuscript there was only one way Brooke could have gotten her hands on it. She had to have swiped it. After all, Brooke had once been a friend of Capote's, and would have been in and out of his homes in Manhattan and the Hamptons numerous times.

So Brooke must have stolen the manuscript to keep it from being published. But why would she hold onto this damning story of an affair that at the time had the power to ruin her and her family with its explicit sex, not to mention the truth about the paternity of her love child? Benedict would have been dead by then, so the only reason Madeline could think of was that Capote's description of the dark, tangled love affair kept the memory of her lost lover alive. A dangerous reason.

It was three thirty in the morning when she stopped reading. Madeline clipped the pages together and slid them back in the envelope.

Had Cecil read the chapter about his mother and the handsome Benedict, who according to the manuscript had murdered an undercover cop to protect his Mafia family? Cecil had been anxious, make that extremely anxious, to find an old manila envelope in his mother's townhouse, so chances were that he had. Of course he'd read it.

But she had it now, and Cecil didn't. Good.

Madeline would decide tomorrow what to do. The manuscript could very well be authentic, but it could be just a parody of Capote's lost novel, a spoof penned long ago by a talented graduate student or something. With no meaning or value. Except, obviously to Brooke.

She thought about Cecil. But what if he ever wondered why the security system had been turned off earlier that night—and decided to download the cameras' video file? Would he see a shadowy figure walking from the kitchen to the hall and out the front door? Would he be able to tell that it was her? And would he suspect that she'd found the missing manuscript? And come after her?

She had to tell Abby what she'd found. She had to tell someone, just in case. Worried, she lay awake for two hours, and then fell into a fitful sleep.

**

Madeline walked into Coda Gems the next day in ripped blue jeans that cost a fortune and sky-blue cowboy boots that cost even more. Late for once, she plopped the manila envelope on Abby's desk.

As Abby watched, Madeline pulled out the manuscript and said, "So, I sort of broke into Brooke's townhouse last night. Looking for this. And I found it before Cecil did. He thought I knew where it was, but of course I didn't."

Abby said, alarmed, "What do you mean 'sort of broke in'?" She stood up.

"You broke into Brooke's home last night?"

Madeline grimaced. "Well yes, although technically all I did was let myself in because I knew where she kept a spare key. So after an hour, well more than an hour, I found this," nodding to the manuscript, "in Brooke's kitchen, in a cabinet, way in the back. So I took it. To keep her damn son Cecil from finding it, because he's a prick. I did it for Brooke."

She told Abby the whole story of Brooke's boxes, and Cecil's intent to turn his mother's papers over to the Boston Public Library. "Especially a missing envelope with old estate records. Or so he told me," said Madeline. "I think he was lying about turning over Brooke's papers to the library. He just needed a good cover story. What he really wanted was to find this." She pointed out Capote's name on the title page of the manuscript, and flipped to the chapter, 'A Brahmin Slut'. "Catchy title isn't it?" she laughed. "Cecil would never, ever have turned this over to any library. I'm sure he just told me that because he needed to have a reason why he was so intent on finding it."

Abby pressed, "So you stole it."

Madeline shrugged. "Whatever. Brooke was friends with Capote years ago, and the main character in this story is her. The woman's background, and the description of her husband…everything fits. It's Brooke. And I think this is Truman Capote's long-lost manuscript, *Answered Prayers.* You have read about it, right? A lot of people have looked for this for years."

Abby arched her eyebrows and reached for the manuscript, but Madeline said, "You shouldn't touch it, not without gloves. Fingerprints you know."

"Yours are all over it."

Madeline held up her hands, in driving gloves. "I don't want you involved in this in any way. Besides, if it's real, Capote's fingerprints are all over it and I don't want them smudged."

"What? This is ridiculous." Abby flipped the pages with the end of a pencil, reading the chapter "A Brahmin Slut," glancing up at Madeline when she got to the explicit sex scenes. Capote, according to what Madeline had read, had been quite good at getting his women friends to confide their deepest secrets. And if this story was true, Brooke had kept nothing back from him. Nothing

70

whatsoever.

When Abby finished the chapter, she looked up. "This is unbelievable! And you think this really is Capote's manuscript? Because if it is, oh my God, this is huge news. This will be a sensation in the media. Headline news." Abby paused, and added, "Along with the juicy revelation that Brooke Sears of *the Boston Sears* committed adultery with a Mafioso and she..."

Madeline interrupted, "You sound like a character out of *The Scarlet Letter*. Adultery isn't what it used to be.

"But what will you do with it?"

"That's the problem," said Madeline. "Nothing. There's nothing I can do, since I don't know if it's authentic. And I'm not about to ask Cecil. He'd kill me. Seriously, he'd kill me. He can never ever know I took this."

Abby thought for a moment and said, "Well, Skinner Auction has a Fine Books and Manuscripts department and I know the woman who heads it. She appraises old manuscripts all the time. I can ask her to take a look at it."

"And what if she says it is authentic? First of all, she'd want to know how I got a hold of it, a problem since I sort of stole it..."

Abby interrupted, "You didn't 'sort of' steal it. You did steal it."

"Well, yes, but technically you can't steal something that's already been stolen."

"What do you mean, technically?" The bell on their front door jangled as a customer came in. Abby stood up. "Hold that thought." She walked out to greet them.

She came back ten minutes later and Madeline said, "If this manuscript is real, then Brooke had to have swiped it from Capote. He'd never have given it to her, since this manuscript was going to make him even more famous than he already was." Madeline shook her head. "No, I absolutely can't show this to any experts. They would call *The New York Times* in a heartbeat if they thought this was the real thing. And of course there would be a media circus, and Brooke's name dragged through the mud. The whole thing would be enough to make her want to die if she weren't already dead."

Madeline ran her fingers through her hair. "Anyway, I thought I'd show it to you. I wanted you to know I found it."

71

"Can't you just mail it back to Cecil, anonymously?"

"No, I won't do that. Cecil is desperate to find it, but I'm the one who did. And I want him to wonder for, well, for forever, where it is. He deserves that. Besides, he's a prick."

"So you said. Which means what, that you're not going to do anything with it?"

"No, I can't. I went looking for it just to keep it out of Cecil's hands. Which I've done. So it won't hurt to just hold onto it. My conscience is clear."

"Your conscience is clear because you rarely use it." Abby sighed. "This manuscript is Pandora's Box, and real or not, it's toxic. But more important, and this is my point, Madeline, it's not yours."

Madeline ignored the comment and said, "I'll keep it in our safe, which is as good a place as any for now." She stuffed the envelope into a larger one and placed it into their biometric, wall-mounted safe. To get inside without a fingerprint a thief would have to have a blowtorch to crack it open, or pry it out of the wall with a lever. That is if they could get into their building, and then through the front door, wired to their security company.

"You know what? I think you should just get rid of it," said Abby. "Why keep it?"

"Brooke could have destroyed it, but she didn't. So I won't either."

Abby said, "So you believe the manuscript is Capote's?"

Madeline shrugged. "I think it probably is. No harm though in just holding onto it. I can do that, just like what Brooke did. Hold onto it."

"Well, I think that is a stupid idea. Actually, a terrible one. I think you're crazy."

"It will be just fine in our safe."

"But I don't think you should just—" began Abby.

"Don't worry about it. Seriously, it'll be fine."

"You know what, I think you're obsessed with Brooke Sears."

"Obsessed? No. But this manuscript is safe with me." A pause and Madeline continued, "So Brooke must have spilled her big secret to Capote and he went and put it in a book for God's sake. No wonder Brooke was so excessively protective of her privacy. No wonder she was paranoid."

"Well, I hope the police find her killer soon," said Abby.

"I know. Me too. What a horrible way for her to die. I can't stop thinking about it. If only there was something I could do."

Abby said, "Well at the very least I'm glad Cecil doesn't know you have it."

Madeline didn't respond, because Abby would not be happy to hear that he just might. And would demand that she get rid of it.

***

At the store the next day Madeline sat at her workbench, staring at her digital microscope and milligram scale, expensive leftovers from her fifteen years as a gem dealer. She couldn't stop thinking about Brooke. She sighed and turned back to the microscope. Who had murdered her? And why? Why? But what she needed to do now was to concentrate on her work. Madeline was a certified gemologist, and handled their customers' jewelry appraisals, as well as all of the buying and most of the auctions, but that morning, when she double-checked her appraisals, she found three mistakes.

To get her mind off Brooke, at the end of the day Madeline dusted off her gym bag and drove to the health club at the Ritz Carlton. It was a good place to meet prospective customers, she'd thought when she'd signed up, even if it did involve actually working out. She'd been to the club two times in the last year. Maybe three.

But hate it or not, she changed into her black swimsuit, and headed to the pool for Aqua Boot Camp which sounded strenuous and exhausting. Perfect. There were ten other women in the class, all younger, and all of them fit. There was one man, burly, muscular, mid-40s, short dark hair shot with gray, who had broad shoulders and a narrow waist. A strong swimmer too. A man who was either unaware of the looks from the women in the class, or didn't care.

In the locker room afterwards, Madeline changed into blue jeans and a red sweater, and slid the eight-carat pink sapphire ring back on her left hand. After all, women in the gem business should wear spectacular jewelry. She walked into the Blue Café, conveniently located in the sports club, and joined a table with her boot-camp classmates. As she pulled out a chair a woman in yellow slacks commented, "Your ring is beautiful."

Madeline said "Thank you," not mentioning it wasn't hers, but on consignment to Coda Gems. They didn't need to know that level of information. "I'm in the business," was all she said, and several women peppered her with questions about gems, and wanted her business card. After half an hour, her fellow swimmers drifted out the door except for the burly man, whose name she learned was John. John Althorp.

"Your pink sapphire is stunning," he said, and Madeline glanced at him. So he knew something about gems. Most people wouldn't have recognized it as a sapphire.

Madeline looked down at her ring. "Yes, it is, isn't it?"

John was pleasant enough, but not her type. She was drawn to lean, intense men, although to be honest that hadn't worked out all that well.

He smiled. "My wife loved pink sapphires. So of course I always knew what to buy for birthdays and anniversaries." He laughed. "She loved pink, said it was the most beautiful color in the world. Everything in her closet was pink. I told her once she dressed like a flamingo and she told me 'Nobody's perfect.'" He had a crinkled smile, lazy and intimate.

The man used past tense, so Madeline assumed his wife had died, since few refer to a former spouse without the 'ex' modifier.

John continued, "She came home once after a trip to London and she'd had her hair dyed pink." He grinned. "Not a hard pink, but a very pale, cotton-candy pink. Which was unnerving." And this time he laughed out loud.

Madeline looked at him. So either the man had murdered his wife and had zero remorse, or it had been an unusually amicable divorce. At the very least, she could be pleasant for a minute or two, and then she would leave. She nodded to the rolled-up yoga mat in his bag. "So, you practice yoga?"

"Let's say I attend a class. You know, I've noticed that very few yoga practitioners are in prison."

"I never thought about that. How do you know?"

He hesitated. "I'm observant."

A waiter came over and John asked if she'd like a drink. She ordered a martini. After all, she had to like a man whose wife dyed her hair pink and he thought it was funny. John reached in his back pocket for his wallet and she saw the butt of a handgun in a shoulder holster under his jacket.

He caught her glance, shrugged, and said, "I'm with the Feds." That was it, no further explanation. She watched as John's eyes flickered across a group of men in their thirties who noisily took a table in the corner. John stood up. "Nice to have met you, but I have to leave."

He dropped several bills on the table and said to a passing waiter, "That should cover our drinks," nodded to her, and walked out, skirting the table of men. In a hurry, his movements precise. Ex-military she decided.

Why did he leave in such an abrupt way and where did he go? Five minutes later she left the bar and drove home, her eyes glancing in the rear-view mirror at a dusty and unremarkable blue Pontiac that had been two cars behind her for the last ten minutes. She took two abrupt right turns and then a left, and lost the car. Maybe she wasn't being followed. But if someone was indeed following her, surely they also knew where she lived. Was Cecil having her followed? Why didn't he just show up with a couple of cops and demand the manuscript?

At least she hadn't thought about Brooke for an hour and a half. Maybe she would go back to the sports club again. Someday.

***

The next morning at ten, the buzzer at Coda Gems rang and in the back office. Abby glanced out, hit the door release, and said to Madeline, "It would seem there's an undertaker come to visit."

Madeline looked out. "That's just Alfred, Brooke's lawyer. He's delivering her pearls. He phoned this morning."

The lawyer walked in, wearing a gray suit, gray tie, and carrying a glossy black briefcase in his hand. They shook hands, Alfred's cold as ice.

"I was going to have the pearls sent to you by a security firm, but since it's Saturday I thought I'd bring them myself. And to apologize in person for that scene with Paige in my office the other day. I'm sorry if you were uncomfortable."

"No problem. Although it was a bit of a drama, wasn't it? Coffee?"

He shook his head, and she led him to her desk in the back.Alfred snapped open his briefcase, and took over a stack of small velvet folders, with jewelry inside. Over the next hour he set each piece of jewelry on Madeline's desk, which she examined, as well as a pearl report from the Gemological Institute, and scrawled her initials on his list.

Then she picked up an old-fashioned, clunky pearl and amethyst necklace that Brooke had once told her had belonged to an old aunt. A necklace Brooke said she cherished. Madeline decided she'd keep that one. After she finished with the last piece of pearl jewelry she said, looking up with a half-smile, "Well, this is all a bit...overwhelming. Alfred, do you know why Brooke left her jewelry to me?"

He set the initialed list in his briefcase. "Unfortunately, I can't discuss any conversations I had with Brooke, even though she is deceased. As you know, she asked me to write an amendment...this was her wish."

"I guess I understand, sort of. How upset is Paige?"

"I can't really talk about that either," said Alfred, and picked up his briefcase. "Let me know if she ever...bothers you."

"Bothers me?" said Madeline.

"Never mind. She'll probably be going back to Los Angles any day. Brooke talked about you, you know. She told me about the auctions you went to together. She enjoyed it. And coming here to your store," he looked around, "and just talking." He stood up. "Dear Brooke. I will miss her every day for the rest of my life. Every single day."

Madeline glanced at him, but Alfred was already walking toward the front door. She followed and he stopped for another cold handshake, then went out the door. She stared after him, a man from another generation.

And a man who had been in love with Brooke.

Madeline went through each of the black folders again, taking out the pieces, then putting each back. Finally, she stood up and opened their safe, easing Capote's manuscript to the back so she could set them inside. They needed a bigger safe.

She and Abby talked for an hour that afternoon about the best way to sell Brooke's pearls. Abby was in favor of going through an auction house or consigning them, but Madeline finally said, "Consignment can take a long time, and going through an auction house, from start to finish, can take up to six months or more. And online auctions can be iffy. I think we should sell Brooke's pearls here, at Coda Gems."

Abby protested. "But Madeline these pieces will be too expensive for our regular customers."

"I know. We'll need to bring in new ones, so we'll advertise. I'll have an ad agency take photos, design an ad, and then we'll run it in *The Boston Globe* and a few suburban papers. And then, just like that," and she snapped her finger, "we'll have new customers blowing through our door."

Abby laughed, "Just what we need, our doors blown off." Madeline didn't say anything, just stared out their glass door. She said to Madeline, "Is something wrong?"

"Sorry, I'm just a bit distracted. Yes, that's what we need, new customers. With money." But Madeline wasn't thinking about a crush of customers, she was thinking about Cecil. He must not have realized she had the manuscript or surely he'd have shown up by now. So she should just stop worrying about him. And focus on selling Brooke's pearls.

***

On Monday morning Cecil took the elevator to the 11th floor of the Federal Building and walked down the beige hallway with cheap beige carpeting to the office of Bruce Friedman, the ranking U.S. senator from Massachusetts. Bruce had sent Cecil at text late the night before that he wanted to talk, and would ten the next morning in his office be convenient?

Cecil had smiled as he had sent off his reply. "Thanks. Sounds good."

Bruce had to have good news about his nomination to the federal bench. If he didn't, Bruce would have just called and given him the bad news over the phone.

Cecil spoke to the quiet woman at the reception desk and a minute later Bruce walked out with a broad smile to meet him. Another good sign. The two men shook hands. The senator, in his late fifties, with a patrician nose and sharp brown eyes under his jet-black eyebrows began, "I was so sorry to hear about your mother."

Cecil nodded. "Thank you. And I appreciate the flowers you sent to the house."

Bruce nodded and ushered him into his office, unremarkable except for the huge state flag of Massachusetts hanging from an eight-foot stand in the corner. He said to Cecil, "No problem. And I know this is a difficult time for you, but I wanted to let you know, in person, that the president will send your formal nomination to the senate judiciary committee on Monday. Congratulations."

Cecil said, pretending surprise, said, "Well, that is wonderful news, Bruce. Just wonderful. Thank you. Thank you for your efforts. I can't tell you how much I—"

Bruce interrupted, "No problem. Of course we'll have to wait for the committee to screen your professional career, and then for the FBI to conduct a background check." Bruce laughed, "Looking for the odd skeleton." He smiled at Cecil.

Cecil grinned, as if that was a hilarious thought.

Bruce cautioned him. "Just remember, with the background checks and the vetting and the confirmation hearings, which I have no doubt you'll sail through, and then the senate vote, the whole thing will take months. It's a long process."

"Yes, I understand. Still, this is such great news. And thank you again."

Bruce checked his watch and stood up. "Sorry, but I have to duck in a meeting and then fly back to Washington in an hour. But I wanted to tell you the good news in person, before I left. I'll be in touch. And congratulations again."

Cecil stood as well, and the two men shook hands.

Back in his car, Cecil turned on the radio, humming to Springsteen's "Born to Run." Of course his nomination to the federal bench would be successful, since he was eminently qualified. But Cecil's plans went beyond that. And eventually, according to his long-term strategy, he'd make it onto the Supreme Court. Where he'd be named chief justice after a couple of years. He was nothing if not ambitious. It was in his DNA.

But Cecil still worried about that old manuscript. He'd let himself into his mother's townhouse early that afternoon when she was late coming back from lunch, and while he'd waited in her study, he picked up an old manuscript lying on her desk. By Truman Capote? Ha-ha, very funny. Flipping through the pages, he stopped dead at the chapter "A Brahmin Slut." He started to skim the story, his heart pounding, then went back to the beginning, taking his time, his heart in his throat. Yes, the woman in that chapter was his mother, no doubt about that. And according to the story, she'd had an affair with a member of the Mafia. His mother? Ridiculous. Impossible. And he read about a baby that Capote called "The First Born."

And he was, unmistakably, that child.

He threw down the manuscript. The whole thing was preposterous, as well as libelous. Henry Sears was not his father? Of course it must be a nasty joke. Then his mother had walked in, and Cecil had waved the manuscript, shouting, "What in God's name is this? Of course this can't be true."

When she had just stared at him, he added, "Or is it?"

Furious, she'd grabbed the pages from his hand, and shouted, "Just leave. Now. Go. And give me your key."

It was an ugly scene.

Later that night the police showed up at Cecil's home to break the news that his mother was dead. After he identified her body at the morgue, he drove back to her townhouse to get the manuscript, but the police were there, collecting evidence. And they told him, politely but firmly, that he had to leave. He waited days before he could get back in.

By now he'd searched her townhouse thoroughly. He'd gone through every shelf in her library, and every drawer, every cabinet, every closet, and the basement too, He even went through her trash bin. The envelope and manuscript were just not anywhere. The only thing he could think of was his mother must have what, burned it in her fireplace?

Cecil sighed again. He should just stop worrying about it.

Just in case, he had turned on the security system when he'd left that day to go to the reading of her will. Or he thought he had turned it on.

His cell phone buzzed and he looked down. A text from Paige. Why couldn't she just go back to Los Angeles? Her message said she had to talk to him in person about something important, and would stop by his office in half an hour. Cecil replied that was fine, but he only had a few minutes to talk, so she needed to be on time.

***

An hour later Cecil was at his desk when his receptionist cracked open his door. "Your sister is here."

Cecil sighed and said, "Fine. Show her in." He checked to make sure there was nothing about his potential nomination on his desk. He guessed it would be announced in the next couple of days, but the less his sister knew about it beforehand the better. With any luck, she would be gone before the news hit the media. Regardless, she was here now and he had to talk to her. He knew what she wanted. Every time he'd seen Paige in the last five years she'd only wanted to talk about money.

His.

Cecil hadn't spoken to his sister since the disastrous reading of the will at Alfred's office. After he'd come back inside after his infuriating conversation with Madeline in the parking lot, Paige had gone on and on for over half an hour, screaming, yelling, threatening to contest. Alfred had told her she had every right to do so. But it would be money wasted. Finally she'd stormed out. Cecil knew he'd hear from her again soon.

A knock sounded on his office door. Paige strode in, wearing her tight jeans, and a low-cut sweater under a leather bomber jacket. Her clothes were way too young for her, but he wasn't about to comment.

She said, "So how are you?"

"Fine." He stood up and kissed her. Paige smelled of cigarettes. And gin. "Just curious, when are you heading back to Los Angeles? Martha and I would like to have you over for—"

"I'm scouting locations for my movie. It would be cheaper to film the establishing ocean shots here. Like on the North Shore. Tax credits, you know. So I'll be here for another three weeks or so."

He forced himself to say, "Well that's good news. By the way, have you picked up Mother's clothes yet?"

Paige made a face and slumped in a chair across from his desk, "Yes, and by the way, the museum has already changed the locks. If you can believe it, I had to make an appointment with them just to get in. Two of them were there, and watched me the whole time, as if they were afraid I was going to rip the damn drapes off the windows or something. I noticed all her books are gone from the library."

"Yes, I had them picked up two days ago."

"What will you do with them?"

He shrugged. "I'll keep her books. Can't hurt to hold onto them."

Paige fiddled with her cell phone and looked at him. "How is Mother's investigation going? I haven't heard a thing from the cops. You talk to them every day, don't you?"

"Well not every day, but almost every day, and there's nothing new. Detective Amick from Homicide has assured me they have three officers on the case. Don't worry, they'll find the person who murdered Mother. Soon, I should think."

Paige sighed and ran her fingers through her hair, her voice trembling. "How could Mother have left all of her pearl jewelry to that blonde tramp? Why would she do that to me?"

Cecil watched her, waiting.

"To cut to the chase, Cecil, I need a loan, just for a couple of months. Can I borrow $250,000?" She smiled and added, "Please? I'll get my trust check from Alfred in four months and I'll…"

Cecil sighed. "I lent you $350,000 two years ago. I'm not a bank. And then there was the time five years ago that you—"

"I wasn't expecting to run so short of money for my new movie. I'm already incurring expenses, and to top it all off, my assistant quit this morning. He

81

didn't even call me, just sent me a text. A text, if you can believe that." She shook her head, "And I can't mortgage my house because it's—"

"Mortgaged to the hilt. I know. You tell me that every time you need a loan. Look, Paige, I can't come up with $250,000. I can't."

He could come up with that kind of money, it just meant moving some investments around, but he wasn't about to. And he didn't want her to turn around and ask him for a smaller amount either so he lied. "All of my money is tied up right now. All of it. I'm in a tough financial spot, too."

Paige stood up, pacing between the door and his desk. "Mother would have lent me the money if she were alive."

"Yes, she probably would have. But unfortunately she's not." He had to be careful. There was a chance the FBI would interview Paige during their background checks for his nomination. And he didn't want her spewing a stream of vitriol if they did.

He asked, his tone solicitous, "How are your headaches? Better I hope?" He wondered if she'd ever had headaches. Paige was an experienced liar.

"Thanks for asking, but I'm fine. Don't worry Cecil, I can't hold out financially for four months. This is a disaster, and I don't know what to do. I've got to go into production as soon as possible. I'm in a horrible jam and you're the only one I know who can save my film from—"

"Maybe Alfred can find a way to give you an advance. I'll ask him to see what he can do."

"I already asked him at that meeting at his office last week. While you were outside talking to that blonde bimbo who has Mother's pearls. And Alfred said no. I told you he hates me. So I'm stuck. I'm desperate. Very desperate."

"I am sorry to hear that."

"You know, this couldn't happen at a worse time. I know, I just know, that my new film will be my commercial break, domestically. And overseas, too, of course. I've already had casting conversations. The lead actor I want was nominated for an Oscar...fifteen years ago, but still. And the script is first-rate. Which, by the way, I wrote. So I'll get a screenwriting credit too."

Cecil didn't ask what her film was about because he didn't want to know. He was sure it would be weird, creepy, and gruesome. A movie where the living and the dead would all end up covered in blood.

Paige added, "There's a couple of scenes in it that are quite funny."

"Well, that's good to hear."

"I was counting on Mother to leave me her jewelry, and I was sure she would throw me a million or so." She looked at Cecil, adding, "And give you a million too of course. She was always fair to us that way."

Cecil nodded, as if that were true. It wasn't. Their mother had always favored Paige in small, subtle ways. Although in ways sometimes not so small and not so subtle, even though Paige had always been a problem.

His secretary knocked, stuck her head in and announced, "Excuse the interruption, but I have London on the line."

Cecil turned and said to Paige. "I really am sorry, but there is nothing I can do. Except like I said, talk to Alfred. Are you still staying with friends?"

She ignored the question and said, "Thanks for talking to Alfred. But can you lend me something now? Anything?" she said, "Like I said, I'm desperate. I've got bills to pay."

Cecil knew he had to give her something, so he pulled a checkbook out of his desk drawer. "I can lend you $25,000, but that's all." He scrawled out a check and handed it to her. She stared at it, probably counting the zeroes, before she stuffed it in her purse, and muttered, "Thanks."

"Remember, that's a loan."

Paige slammed her way out of his office.

He didn't pick up his phone after Paige left, because London wasn't on the line. He'd told his secretary to interrupt him with that message after his sister had been in his office for five minutes.

Cecil dropped the checkbook back in his drawer and paced his office. He was worried that the FBI might turn up old rumors from twenty-five years ago, when he was at the D.A.'s office and Paige a senior at Wellesley. When her best friend, or rather her ex-best friend, died at a party in Chelsea after falling from a fifth-floor roof deck. According to Paige, the only witness, "Alexandra tripped and lost her balance, and there was nothing I could do. It was awful, just awful."

But at the time Cecil didn't think it was an accident, and neither did his mother. And then a second witness showed up, a homeless man who was digging in a dumpster in the alley across the street that night. The man claimed he'd seen two women who looked like they were arguing on the edge of the roof. He said he saw a woman with short, black hair shove the victim off the roof, and watched her fall to the sidewalk five stories below. He'd been interviewed by police three times, his story never changing. The police requested criminal charges be filed against Paige, but Cecil knew the clerk magistrate in Chelsea, and asked him for a favor. In the closed-door hearing the magistrate declined to issue criminal charges against Paige, and the woman's death ended up classified as accidental. But just to be sure, Cecil had Alfred track down the homeless man and made him disappear. After all, Alfred knew people who knew people. Cecil was aware that afterwards there had been talk that he had been behind the clerk magistrate's surprising decision, and even the disappearance of the homeless man.

Hopefully that wouldn't come up in his background check. It was a long time ago after all. Still, the last thing Cecil needed at this stage of his nomination was even a hint of tampering with criminal court proceedings, much less a whisper of a link to the disappearance of a witness. Especially when there was an ongoing murder investigation of his mother's death for God's sake. He'd been so sure Paige would fly back to Los Angeles right after their mother's funeral. Too bad she'd be around for another two or three weeks. But there wasn't much he could do about that.

Cecil pulled open the bottom drawer of his desk and took out a bottle of Lisinopril for his high blood pressure. He blamed his tour in Afghanistan between college and law school for that, a dusty, dirty, medieval and brutal country where the Taliban wounded him twice. He still had nightmares.

He frowned as he fiddled with his cell phone. His secretary walked in again, and said, "Senator Friedman's office is on the line. He wants to talk about a press release from his office."

Cecil took the call.

***

The next morning, already on her second cup of coffee at her desk, Madeline read *The Boston Globe*. On page four of the Metro Section, a page she almost skipped, was a press release from Senator Friedman's office, regarding a new nomination to the federal bench, for none other than Cecil Sears.

"*Yesterday, U.S. Senator Bruce E. Friedman announced the President of the United States has nominated Cecil J. Sears to serve as a judge in the United States District Court for the District of Massachusetts. Cecil is a Harvard and Yale educated, Boston-bred litigator, and a partner of the law firm Sears Taylor & Yost, LLP. Senator Friedman laid out several reasons why Sears would be an excellent judge, citing his tremendous legal background, a proven commitment to serve the Boston community, and his ten years in private practice, as well as his decorated service as a Marine in Afghanistan.*"

The press release went on to list Cecil's litigation experience, his affiliations as Appellate Practice faculty member at both the Harvard School of Law and the Yale School of Law, and his experience in state and appellate courts at all levels, including the US Supreme Court.

Bully for him, thought Madeline. A lifetime of stellar accomplishment even if it did sound deadly boring. It was the word 'deadly' that made her sit up.

Because at that moment it was as if a bolt of lightning had crashed through the office window. A red-hot bolt of lightning. Madeline stared at the safe. Inside was a powerful motive for murder. Several of them actually. Forget about the explicit sex and the fact that Brooke had consorted with a known Mafia member in the chapter "A Brahmin Slut." *What if the part about an illegitimate child was actually true?* A child Capote nicknamed 'The First Born.' That would be Cecil of course, arrogant and proud of the Sears name. A name that he had no legal right to, along with the income from the huge trust fund Henry Sears set up for his children. After all, wouldn't the trustees of the Sears's family trust be obligated to remove Cecil as a beneficiary if he was not legally Henry's son? Paige would certainly have a case that Cecil's share of the trust fund should revert to her.

In addition, there would be a tremendous scandal if Cecil J. Sears was not at all who he seemed to be. Not the scion of the venerable Sears family, but rather the son and grandson of ruthless Mafia criminals, a family steeped in homicide, drugs, and gambling. The scandal alone would crater Cecil's chances of a senate confirmation to the federal bench. He had everything to lose if the manuscript ever saw the light of day and his true paternity exposed. Everything. Kaput.

Which would explain his obsession about finding the missing envelope.

And what if Cecil decided that in order to squash the truth of his paternity, he also had to silence his own mother? Permanently? Had he murdered Brooke to protect himself from total ruin?

She sighed. There was no question now that she had to take the manuscript to the police, and get them to focus their attention on Cecil. Even if that meant Brooke's personal life would be exposed to scorn and her privacy eternally shattered. Brooke would have hated that, but Madeline couldn't let Cecil get away with murder.

Except the manuscript wasn't evidence. The police would listen to her, read the chapter on Brooke, and ask her the dicey question of how it had come into her possession. And then they'd talk to Cecil. Who could of course say the manuscript was his mother's joke, and insist it be returned to him, and accuse Madeline of burglary. Which also meant she'd have Cecil on her doorstep, ready to come after her with his prosecutorial guns at the ready. If the woman in the story really was Brooke

Had the police asked Cecil where he was the night of Brooke's murder? She was sure they had, so he must have a good alibi. But alibis can be discredited. All she had to do was get Detective Amick to suspect Cecil's was a lie.

Madeline went to the coffee maker and poured herself another cup.The first thing she had to do was find out if the story about Brooke and her Mafia lover and their child was true. Once she knew that, well *then,* she could take the manuscript to the police and they'd have to thoroughly investigate Cecil. At that moment she remembered the third best source that Felix her ex-husband, the investigative reporter, had mentioned years ago. He'd said, 'The Source Store.' Whatever that meant. She should have asked him.

Madeline pulled the manuscript out of the safe, making notes of exactly what Capote had written about Benedict's crime family. His father was a bloodthirsty don, according to Capote, who'd murdered two members of a rival family with his bare hands, and had ordered the execution of seven others. But the name of the crime family was never mentioned. Still, it made sense that the family was probably based in New England, since the woman was originally a Boston Yankee and only lived in Manhattan after she married.

Not a lot to go on, but it was something. Since she had to start somewhere, she googled "New England Mafia families" and came up with a list of nine that were active in the 60's and 70's. Which was not all that helpful.

She had to talk to someone in law enforcement. Well there was Detective Amick, but she was a hard-assed woman who treated her like she was already a prime suspect. There was John Althorp, a man who said he worked with the Feds, who she'd met at the health club. He carried a gun so he probably was in federal law enforcement of some kind. And he liked her. So yes, John was her man, in a manner of speaking.

***

Madeline went to her swimming class that night at her sports club, hoping John would be there. He was. When her class met at Blue Cafe afterwards, she made sure she sat next to him. She wore the pink sapphire again, and talked with him about pink sapphires until the other women left.

John ordered seltzer water, and Madeline did the same. He said, nodding to her left hand, "You know that's the kind of ring my wife Ann would have loved."

Past tense again, so the woman was definitely dead.

"Yes, it is a beautiful ring," she said. "I'm lucky."

John shrugged. "Ann loved jewelry, and horses. Then she gave everything away. All of it. Says she's happier now."

Which didn't sound to Madeline like she was all that dead. She looked at him.

"She's a Catholic nun now, a missionary. In Rwanda."

"Really? A nun? That's unusual."

"She's an unusual woman. Bull-headed too. We were married for seven years. No kids. Did you ever see the movie *African Queen* with Katherine Hepburn and Humphrey Bogart? Ann is just like the character Hepburn played in that movie. Strict. No nonsense. Determined." He shrugged. "Anyway, she left me and joined the convent, so I guess I wasn't a good enough Bogart." Sadness flashed across his face.

After the waiter came with their drinks, she told John she owned a jewelry store in Downtown Crossing but would be moving to a better location soon. He told her he had been born and raised in South Boston, and had always lived there. "Except for five years when I was in the Marines."

"So what do you do now?"

"I'm a special agent with the DEA."

Perfect. Or sort of perfect. Madeline hesitated, not sure how to bring up the subject of New England Mafia crime family history. She asked John about his job at the DEA.

"It's mostly computer work, looking for money laundering activity." John glanced up, smiling, "Which I guess means I'm basically an armed CPA."

An opening for Madeline. "How very interesting. Have you ever done any work investigating the Mafia? Do you know anything about the Mafia in Boston? The old Mafia families, I mean. About forty-five years ago or so?"

John laughed. "The Mafia? Forty years ago?"

"I'm doing research on an old story," she said. "And, well, I need to talk to someone in law enforcement about New England crime families. In the 1970's. I have to check out gossip from back then. I don't know how to go about that."

John arched his eyebrows. "Gossip?"

Madeline laughed. "Yes. Old rumors about crime families."

He stared at her. "You're writing a book?"

"Well, no. I have an old manuscript, and I want to find out if one of the stories in it is true. That's all."

"And it's important? Obviously, or you wouldn't have asked."

"Yes. It's important."

"That's not my area. Sorry."

"No worries. Just thought I'd ask."

"Where did you get this manuscript?"

"From a friend," she lied. Well, it was only sort of a lie. "It might have a bearing on a…crime."

"What kind of crime?"

"A homicide."

John looked up, interested. "A recent homicide?"

"Well, yes."

"And who wrote this story?"

"Someone who died years ago."

"And you want to know if it's true. But the only way you can verify it is through…old rumors you say?"

Madeline nodded, "Yes, old rumors."

John smiled. "You're talking about unsubstantiated information. Well, you'd definitely be better off with the state police or the Boston police rather than the DEA. So what kind of rumors?"

Madeline sighed. "About an illegitimate child."

John, laughed. "That's a bit outside of their usual…purview."

"I would imagine. But still, someone may have heard something. And remembered."

"And it's connected to a current homicide you say? Male or female?"

She corrected him. "One that *may* be connected. To the murder of a woman."

Their waiter came up and Madeline gave him her credit card. He was back in a minute and she signed the receipt. "Basically, I need to talk to someone who's familiar with the Boston Mob of forty years or so ago."

"Well, you have an interesting story, and I'm curious now, too. I'll see if I can find someone for you to talk to. To be honest, this will be tough, so no promises."

Madeline smiled. "I really appreciate any help. And thank you. It would be wonderful if you could let me know what you find as soon as possible. Sorry, but I need to find someone who knows about the Mafia, right away. It's a long story, but it means a lot to me, Really, a lot. I can't tell you how much." Her smile was shaky now. At least she hoped it was on-the-verge-of-tears-shaky.

John sat up straighter, and Madeline felt bad about playing the damsel in distress card. But it was for a good cause.

"I'll see what I can do. I'll see what I can come up with for you."

As they walked out the door John said, "Can I give you a lift somewhere?"

She shook her head, thanked him, and headed to the garage and to her car on the third level. Once she was out on the street, she kept checking her rear-view mirror, but no one seemed to be following her, as far as she could tell.

She was glad she now had a contact in law enforcement. One who was on her side.

Which was progress.

***

At the store the next morning, Madeline told Abby she thought Cecil had murdered Brooke. And why. And also why she couldn't show Capote's manuscript to the police. Madeline continued, "But I will. Hopefully soon. I'm just…checking into some things."

"You can't be serious," said Abby sitting at her desk and staring at Madeline. "You really are obsessed with Brooke Sears, and now, even worse, you're going after Cecil Sears of all people? All because of this old manuscript?"

"Possibly, yes. I mean definitely yes."

"But Madeline, why? Why would you do that? What proof do you have?"

"I'm not looking for proof, that's up to the police. I'm just looking to establish motive. And Cecil had one. Well, actually two. Big ones. All I need to do is prove that he had a strong motive and then the cops will have to thoroughly investigate him, take his alibi apart and then find the proof that he murdered his mother."

Abby slammed her calculator off. "Madeline, this is crazy. Seriously crazy. You know what I think? I think you've gone off the deep end."

"I haven't. But you see, I have to do something."

"Why? In God's name why?"

"Regret."

"That's a ridiculous reason."

"It happens to be the truth."

A pause, and Abby said, "What you're doing, it isn't dangerous, is it?"

"Of course not. I'm just talking to people, that's all. Having conversations."

"I wish you'd never found that damn manuscript. You should not be involved in a murder investigation at all. You need to keep out of this. It's not your business."

"I'm really not doing that much."

"Madeline, keep out of the Sears's business."

"The only thing I can do for Brooke now is make sure the police take a good, hard look at Cecil as a suspect. That's all I have to do. Then I'm done, finished."

"You make it sound so easy. And safe. But Madeline, you're now on the hunt for a murderer. Not exactly a safe thing to do now, is it?"

Madeline shrugged. "It's safe enough."

***

At the store just after eleven the next morning, the head of the management company for the Jewelers' Building, Paul Davis, showed up at Coda Gems. He was a heavy-set man in his late sixties. Sometimes he was kind and grandfatherly, but usually not. This was definitely a not day.

He looked around when Abby buzzed him in. "I'm following up on your relocation progress. Just checking that you'll be cleared out in six months with all of your display cases, and furniture and whatnot. Totally cleared out. And of course I expect your rent will continue to be paid, on-time, until you leave and—"

"And you're implying exactly what Paul?" Madeline interrupted."That we won't continue to pay our rent on time, every month? We've never been late. Or are you suggesting we'll try and sneak out at the end, owing you money? You've been sitting on our security deposit for two years, which, when we move out, you'll return to us, with interest. That's the law."

91

Paul sniffed. "You don't need to tell me the law."

"I think maybe I do," said Madeline. "Whatever. Don't worry, we'll be moved out before our lease expires. And don't bother us again without a good reason, or I'll make a harassment complaint."

Paul looked around again. "I expect to find the space in perfect condition after you leave." He stalked out.

After he left, Abby looked at Madeline, eyebrows raised. Madeline said, "Well, he was being offensive, and I couldn't let him get away with that." Abby shook her head. "But don't worry, we'll sell a piece of Brooke's pearls soon, I'm sure any day now, and we'll find a great place and then we'll move. And like I said, I'll cover the rent for the first year or so. Speaking of which, we should get a jump on things and start to look at spaces on the upper end of Newbury Street. The way upper end."

Abby looked at her. "There's a difference between getting carried away and leaping off a precipice. Retail spaces there would be too pricey for us. We do need to be reasonable."

"I hate reasonable. Anyway, if we're going to do this, we should do it right. And Newbury Street would be great. Seriously. Just the right area for us to be. So let's go for it."

"That would be...well, that would be a dream come true." Abby smiled and turned away, brushing a tear away from her eye. Which made Madeline determined to find a retail space right smack dab on the corner of Newbury Street and the Boston Public Garden.

Why not? She had, or would have, the money soon. Maybe.

Chapter 6

When Madeline woke up the next morning, she checked her cell phone before she got out of bed. Maybe John Althorp had sent her a text? No text from John. She was being unrealistic. Of course he'd need time. Too bad he couldn't move faster.

Later, as she unlocked Coda Gems, she picked up a package from the ad agency leaning against their front door. Inside were three glossy mock-ups of black and white photos of Brooke's pearls. Abby walked in at nine. Madeline handed her the one on top and said, "My favorite."

Abby looked at the 4-color photo of Brooke's Art Deco pearl necklace and the huge diamond pendant, the pearls spilling out of a black velvet box, with more necklaces, bracelets, and rings, a gleaming jumble off to the side. The Coda Gems' logo was centered underneath.

"What about the copy?"

Madeline said, "What do you think of 'Cartier and Tiffany Pearl Jewelry. One-of-a-kind estate-level pieces.' With our names, address and phone number underneath. Nice and simple."

"That sounds great, Madeline. Perfect actually."

Madeline called the ad agency. "We love the photo of the big necklace! It's fabulous. Really great. Just drop in the copy I'm sending over and email me a PDF along with an insertion order. I'll want to run it in *The Boston Globe*, and online too starting on Monday. And the six suburban papers I mentioned. Every day for the next two weeks, through Sunday."

She hung up and turned to Abby. "This should rustle up some business."

Abby grinned, and hesitating, said, "And you don't think it's too soon? For us to be selling Brooke's pearls I mean. It might seem…callous?"

"No, it will be fine. Nobody will know they were hers."

Abby said, "You're probably right."

Madeline and Abby spent Saturday and Sunday at the store, getting Brooke's pearls ready, arranging her jewelry in the front display case, changing the layout four times, laughing and talking like in the old days when they'd first opened Coda Gems.

***

At 5:45 a.m. on Monday Madeline opened the morning's *Boston Globe,* and called Abby. She knew Abby would be up, the woman kept farmers' hours. "Our ad is on page three no less, and it looks wonderful! This will be a great day! I hope."

They met at the store at 7:30, and again went over the display of Brooke's pearl jewelry in the front glass case, the price tags small and discrete. They had to be. The price of Brooke's pearl pieces was more than a couple of notches above their usual merchandise.

The first customer showed up at 8:30, and by 5:30 that afternoon almost seventy customers had walked through their door to look at Brooke's pearls. A lot of interest, but of their fifteen sales, none were for Brooke's pearls.

As they were starting to close up Abby said to Madeline, "Maybe we should talk about lowering the prices?"

Madeline sighed. "You could be right, but let's wait and see." She took Brooke's big pearl necklace to the back room and set it in the safe. As she walked back to the front of the store, Paige, in black leather pants and a bolero jacket walked in.

Paige said to Madeline, "Is this a good time? If not, I can come back some other time and—"

"No, you're fine, this is fine." Although she wasn't sure if it was all that fine. Why was Paige here? Madeline steeled herself for an ugly scene.

"I happened to see your ad for a collection of Cartier and Tiffany pearls in *The Globe.* My mother's pearls. So I guess Alfred already gave them to you.

You aren't wasting any time selling them, are you?" She paused, and there was an uncomfortable silence before Paige continued. "And of course I could hardly miss her Art Deco necklace with the diamond pendant. You know my father gave her that necklace the night before their wedding. Anyway, I'd like to see it again, just to take a last look, before it's sold. If you don't mind." She smiled.

Madeline had never seen Paige smile. She'd only met Paige twice before, the first time she'd been weeping and the second time shouting.

Paige walked along the front glass case, with Brooke's gleaming pearls gleaming against black velvet, "But I don't see the necklace here." She spun around, facing Madeline, her eyes hard. "You haven't sold it already have you? Don't tell me it's been sold!"

"No. I just put it in the back, but I'm happy to bring it out."

"Good. And thank you."

Madeline went in back and whispered to Abby, "Brooke's daughter is here. Paige. She saw our ad, and wants to see Brooke's pearl necklace. The big one."

Abby said, whispering now too, "Here? You're kidding? Is she upset?"

"Actually no."

"Well that's good. Maybe she wants to buy it."

Madeline hesitated, "Could be. Why not? She certainly has the money."

"So what's the problem?"

"No problem, I guess. So far. I haven't told her we're selling it for $170,000."

Because the necklace was so expensive, they hadn't put a price tag on it, and agreed to discuss price only with serious buyers. Still, Paige made her nervous, so Madeline wasn't about to bring up the price. Yet. Madeline took the necklace from the safe and walked out to the front, spreading it out on a black velvet cloth, centering the eleven-carat diamond pendant. Paige fingered the pendant. "You know, my mother only wore this on special occasions. Very special occasions."

"I should think so," said Madeline.

Paige shot her a look. "My mother did have a bit of the 'To the Manor Born' attitude, didn't she?" Paige sighed. "It was the way she was brought up." She picked up the necklace, and said, "May I?"

"Of course." Madeline set a mirror in front of her, and went behind Paige to hook the strands of pearls around her neck.

Paige stared at her reflection, a glitter of tears in her eyes as she patted the pendant. She looked up at Madeline. "My mother was an extraordinary woman who lived in a strait-laced time. Perhaps 'stifled' is a better term than 'strait-laced'? She was a bit of a born hell-raiser. Or rather could have been, given the opportunity."

Madeline only smiled.

With a flick of her wrist Paige unhooked the clasp. "Thank you. I wish Alfred had stopped Mother from…" she paused, then continued, "I hope you find a good buyer for this necklace. One who treasures it."

"No worries. Our customers have an appreciation of quality."

Paige locked eyes with Madeline in the mirror as she handed her the necklace, "I hope whoever murdered my mother is arrested soon. It makes me uncomfortable that he's still out there somewhere. Walking around."

"I know. It should happen soon, I should think."

Paige watched as Madeline slid the necklace into its velvet case. "Mother used to keep her pearls in a safe deposit box at her bank."

Madeline nodded, "I used to go back and forth to the bank with her pearls three or four times a month when she wanted to wear one of them to an event. Or wherever."

"Mother was always quite careful about her jewelry. She obviously trusted you."

"Well, we did spend a fair amount of time together. Talking about, well, talking about everything."

Paige glanced around the store. "I'm curious; did my mother ever talk about me?"

"About you? No, she never did, or Cecil either for that matter. She was a very private woman, which of course you know. She liked to talk about upcoming jewelry auctions, books, politics. She had opinions."

"Well, she talked about you, all the time," said Paige.

Madeline was surprised. "She did?"

"She said she depended on you, that you were always there for her. But then I was three thousand miles away, wasn't I? Far away. There really wasn't much I could do for Mother. Anyway, there isn't a price tag on the necklace. How much are you selling it for?"

Madeline said, not looking at Paige. "We haven't finalized that yet. We're waiting on a couple of appraisals."

With a wan smile, Paige stood up. "Well, thank you for your time," and walked out the door.

Madeline went to the back room and said to Abby, "Well that was bizarre. Paige seemed almost normal. Sad, but normal. Anyway, she just wanted to see her mother's necklace again. I didn't tell her the price."

"You know what, maybe we…well you…should sell Brooke's pearls through consignment with a dealer? In another city, far away. Like Chicago, or Los Angeles?"

"I think Paige just wanted to see the necklace one last time. If she was interested in buying it she would have said so. God knows she has the money."

But Madeline was uneasy as she and Abby ran through their nightly inventory of their jewelry stock and set them back in the safe. Maybe selling Brooke's pearls themselves was not such a good idea.

***

An hour later Madeline walked in the dark to the parking garage two blocks from the store, her purse slung over her shoulder. She rode the elevator to the top floor, the only level with a parking space that morning. Now the top level was empty. Totally empty.

Normally this wouldn't have bothered her, but it did this time.She clutched her purse close to her and didn't look behind as she walked to her car, the sound of her cowboy boots on the cement echoing in the garage. She clicked open the lock and jumped in. In her rear-view mirror, she thought she saw someone duck behind a pillar but wasn't sure. It could have been her imagination. She sped down the ramp, jammed in her parking pass, and zoomed onto the street.

But she didn't head home. Instead, she drove around the perimeter of the garage three times, looking for someone skulking. Which was ridiculous. Criminals only skulked in bad movies. She was being paranoid. That's what comes from being involved in a murder investigation, even though she wasn't really involved. Well yes, she was involved, given the fact that she was sitting on a big-time motive, but all she was actually doing we waiting for John Althorp to get back to her.

***

Three blocks later at a long red light she sent John a text, "Just checking. Apologies. Know it's too soon. Any gossip info?"

He pinged her back. "Call me when you have a second."

She pulled over and called him.

John said, "I just spoke to Rebecca, a woman I know at the state police. And she said she can't help with any old Mafia information."

"She can't help?"

"Correct. She did ask her boss, who's been there for years, and he told her to not pursue it. Hauling in any of their sources just to check on ancient 'hearsay' would be a waste of time. Rebecca said she'd need something more…substantial before she could go back to him."

Madeline slumped against her seat. "Substantial?"

"Yes. Solid information."

Madeline sighed and ran her fingers through her hair. "I'll do more checking, and as soon I have something, I'll call you. If you don't mind."

"No problem. Maybe we can have a drink next week and talk about your search?"

"Of course. I'll get back to you."

But she had no intention of ever calling John. He was helpful and well-meaning, but she was a long way from having 'solid' information for the state police. Or any law enforcement agency. Until she did, the man was a waste of time. Nice enough, but not her type.

She stared out the windshield, depressed. So looking for old Mafia gossip through the DEA had not been her best idea. Which meant she had to find a better one. She started her car.

***

At Coda Gems the next day, minutes after Abby had left for a meeting in Concord, the door buzzer sounded and Madeline walked out to the front. And there on the other side of the plate glass door stood Felix, her ex-husband.

In the flesh.

Staring back at her was the investigative reporter extraordinaire she'd been married to for four years. Felix had moved from Boston to Chicago three years ago, after they'd put their house on the market and he'd packed up his clothes, his Bose sound system, his opera CD's, and four boxes of computers and iPads. And that was that. She hadn't seen or spoken to him since. Regardless, he was now standing on the other side of the door, tanned and handsome, his pale blue eyes more piercing than she remembered. He was in blue jeans and a white shirt, his blonde hair just touching his collar. He looked thin.

Felix watched her through the glass door with his familiar cool, blue-eyed look and a half smile.

She opened the door and he said, "Sorry to just drop by. Are you surprised?"

"That's one way of putting it."

She stared at him, looked away, and then back again. Not sure where to look.

"Do you have a few minutes?" he asked.

Madeline decided she had a minute. "Yes, come in." After all, it wasn't every day an ex-husband showed up out of the blue.

He walked in and she hung an "Out to Lunch" sign on the door, locked it, and turned to Felix. She was nine years older than Felix, which before they married, he'd said wasn't an issue. Hard to tell now if he'd been honest.

When they were married, he'd been on *The Boston Globe's* Spotlight team, a small group of investigative reporters whose mission, according to Felix, was, "To uncover malfeasance, hold the powerful accountable, and give voice to those who need one." He loved to say that, and always smiled when he did, but he was dead serious. The Spotlight team won a Pulitzer the second year they were married, a year she barely saw him. He promised the next year would be better, but it wasn't. By the fourth year their marriage was over.

She led Felix to the office in back. "So why are you here?"

He still walked like a cat. A predatory cat. Some things never change.

A mocking smile from Felix. "Do you mean why have I shown up at your place of business, or why am I in Boston?"

She sat behind her desk, and looked him in the eye. All she felt at that precise moment was bitterness. Push comes to shove, bitter trumps sad every time. "Both while you're at it."

He pulled out a chair and sat across from her. "To see you. And to let you know I'm back at *The Globe* now." He leaned forward, his blue eyes soft for once. When they had been married empathy had not been a strong point.

Madeline said, "And exactly why do you want to see me? Just curious."

"Mistakes were made..." He hesitated, and started over. "I want to tell you I'm sorry, and to ask for your forgiveness."

Which wasn't like Felix. At all. So either he had just joined AA. Or he was dying.

"Felix, if you've come to ask for a kidney, the answer is no."

He shook his head and started to reach for her hand, but stopped. "Very funny. You were always very funny."

So three years after their marriage had come to a dismal end he shows up and tells her she's funny? Annoyed, she said, "So you're back at *The Globe*?"

Felix nodded. "Yes, I'm back. They offered me a job as their Senior Deputy Managing Editor of Digital Platforms, and, well, who could say no to a job title that long? Besides I was tired of the grind of reporting." He leaned back in his chair, "I've been back in Boston for a month now. Anyway, I saw an ad yesterday for pearl jewelry in our online edition and there, big and bold, was your name and address. So I decided to drop by. Before we just ran into each other in a restaurant or at some charity event in Boston, or whatever, which would be awkward."

She looked at him. "And this isn't awkward?"

"Good point." He hesitated again. "I was afraid if I called that you'd hang up on me. So I decided to come, in person."

She'd known what Felix was like before they were married. He was a man who took phone calls in the shower. There were times he would leave home to follow up on a tip, and she could never be sure when he would be back; it might be a couple of hours or a couple of days. Too many times. A leopard can't change its spots, and she'd lost her interest in exotic felines.

Madeline didn't say anything, and after a long, silent minute Felix stood up, "Well, I'm glad we got this part over." When Madeline didn't respond Felix continued, "Maybe we can talk again sometime?" He pulled a business card out of his wallet and set it on her desk.

Then like a puff of smoke, he was gone.

Madeline sat, unmoving, and waited until she heard their front door open and close. She picked up Felix's business card and dropped it in the wastebasket.

***

The next day at Coda Gems, Abby sold one of Brooke's pearl and platinum bracelets. Madeline had been at her desk in back, haggling with a New York dealer over a gold Rolex when she heard a customer come in and could hear Abby talking to a man for at least half an hour. And then she heard their front door open and close.

Abby walked in the back right after, with a big grin. "Guess what? I just sold Brooke's Cartier Akoya bracelet, the one with five strands. For $35,000!"

"What? You're kidding!" and Madeline stood up. "You did? Really? You sold it?"

Abby laughed, "I swear to God, the man read the appraisal and the pearl report about ten times, slowly, very slowly, asked at least twenty questions, and then handed me his black American Express card. And that was that. The charge was approved, I put the bracelet in a velvet box, he said 'Thank you,' and left."

Madeline hugged Abby and kissed her on the cheek. "This is amazing.

Seriously amazing. I was afraid it might take weeks, maybe months to sell anything. So what was he like?"

"A businessman, in his late fifties, dark suit and tie, black overcoat, short brown hair, wearing a Rolex watch." Abby laughed, "I sound like an eye witness don't I?"

"You know what, this means we can start to look for a new space right away. The 'serious' kind of look, where we're ready to put money down."

"Well, we're not quite there yet. We need more than one sale of Brooke's pearls before we're ready to look at any—"

"I don't agree. We should begin today. Now. Today." She picked up the phone and called Lynne, a real estate broker friend and five minutes later Lynne emailed her a list of available retail spaces and their monthly rents. All on the upper end of Newbury Street, all posh. All expensive.

Madeline handed the list to Abby who looked at it. "You know Madeline we'd need at least three new customers like Brooke to make any of these financially viable, in the long-term."

Madeline said, "But I thought you'd be happy about relocating there."

Abby's eyes narrowed. "I would be happy. Thrilled, actually. But that doesn't mean I've lost my power of reason. These spaces are all too expensive. We should find a space on the other end of Newbury Street, closer to Massachusetts Avenue. With reasonable rents."

"Well, yes, we could. But the best way to get rich customers is to be in a location where rich people go. And besides, I already said I'd cover the rent for the first year or so."

"Which is incredibly generous. But to be honest, you don't have that kind of money yet. And what if we move there and business is not great, and we're stuck with paying an astronomically high rent? There is no way we should move now to an expensive location. We need to be cautious, since who knows what will happen?"

"But I'd rather take that risk. I don't want to live life low-key. I say we do it."

For the next hour, the two partners each sketched out 'pie-in-the-sky' revenue forecasts, based on increased foot traffic minus expenses. Abby's were low and Madeline's were high. So Abby ran two sets of numbers.

"Let's go with my figures," said Madeline, "because they prove we can afford any of these places. We can do it."

Which annoyed Abby. "Well, I am your business partner and I don't agree. We have to be realistic."

And with that, the joy over the bracelet sale vanished.

Madeline shoved the real estate list in a bottom drawer. Making someone else's dream come true was not as easy as one would think. Abby was right, they didn't have the money. Yet. So she wouldn't bring up moving to Newbury Street again for a little while.

At least Abby hadn't asked her about Brooke's murder investigation.

***

But Abby did ask her the next day as she was going through their bills. Madeline didn't look at Abby as she said, "I haven't heard anything new from the police. But I'm following up on a number of angles. Just checking around you know."

Abby slammed a folder of invoices down on her desk. "Following up on a number of angles in Brooke's murder? You're still involved in that? Let me say this one more time, I think you're crazy to try and solve it."

"I'm not trying to solve it, I just want the police to focus on Cecil as the primary suspect. That's all."

The front door buzzer rang, and Abby walked out to the front, saying over her shoulder, "So why are you wasting your time? Why don't you just cut to the chase—and drop the police a few hints?"

Madeline bristled, picked up the phone to call Detective Amick, and set it back down. Drop a few hints? Like she should tell the 'chews-nails-for-breakfast' detective, "You know, I do wonder who Cecil Sears's father really is. Why don't you check into that?"

Alibis, she needed to raise the question of alibis, so she picked up the phone again. When Detective Amick came on the line Madeline began, "This is Madeline Lane, and I'm curious how Brooke Sears's investigation is proceeding?"

"There is nothing new. We're evaluating the evidence and exploring a number of different angles. These investigations take time."

"So are you still assuming it was an interrupted burglary-in-progress?" And then Madeline took the plunge, "Maybe it was someone in Brooke's family who murdered her?" And she grimaced. She hadn't meant to phrase it quite like that.

There was a dead silence before the detective said, "Do you have information that her family might have been involved?" Blunt. Cold. Madeline shouldn't have called.

"No, I don't, I was just curious. About alibis, that kind of thing. I was just curious about Cecil's alibi."

Detective Amick said, "I really can't discuss that. However, I do appreciate your call, and don't hesitate if you think of anything that might be helpful to the investigation. I'm sorry, but I have to cut this short." And she hung up.

Madeline stared at the phone. Well, that was a mistake. The detective hadn't sounded sorry. Madeline was getting nowhere. And she was out of plans. Besides, hadn't she done enough for Brooke already? The question really was—should she still be involved with the Sears family, the living as well as the dead? Maybe she should just drop it.

Which was pretty easy, since all she'd have to do was nothing.

***

Detective Amick sat at her desk, thinking about Madeline's call and her heavy-handed attempt to shift suspicion to Cecil.

She'd talked to Cecil half an hour ago, who had been helpful, as usual. When she'd asked him about his mother's will he had said he would email her a PDF. The detective checked her computer, and an email from Cecil popped up, with an attachment. She opened the document and scanned Brooke's trust and will documents, but stopped when she got to the pearl jewelry amendment. The detective read through it three times, slowly. She picked up the phone and called Cecil, who answered on the first ring.

She said, "Detective Amick here. Thanks for sending your mother's documents. Quick question. What is the approximate value of the jewelry your mother left to Madeline Lane?"

"My sister Paige said about a million dollars, but she tends to exaggerate. So I'm guessing they're worth around $800,000. Give or take."

"This amendment is dated a couple of months ago. A very recent decision."

Cecil said, "Yes. It was a surprise. To me and to Paige."

"I see. Well, thank you." And the detective hung up.

So Brooke had changed her will less than three months before she was murdered, making Madeline a significant beneficiary. Very, very interesting. An $800,000 inheritance was a nice big fat motive for murder. But motive wasn't evidence.

The detective sighed. Her contacts on the street still hadn't been able to provide any information on the murder of Brooke Sears. She still had no solid leads much less an eyewitness, or any forensic evidence that was helpful. She should go through Brooke's boxes that were stacked in the evidence room, and wasn't looking forward to it. A likely waste of time, but it had to be done. The detective pursed her lips. She had already wasted time and resources waiting for Madeline to do something stupid, like driving to a river and tossing in the murder weapon. Maybe the woman was just waiting for the heat to die down.

Regardless, Madeline had more to gain than anyone else by Mrs. Sears's death. So the detective picked up the phone, and called Officer Baxter. "I want another officer on the Madeline Lane surveillance. Right away." At least she hadn't said "Pronto" this time.

The detective sent off a quick update to the superintendent that Brooke had left Madeline $800,000 of jewelry in her will, so she'd ordered an increase in surveillance. And that she'd wait a few days and see what they turned up, then bring in Madeline for questioning again.

It was about time she got this damn investigation moving in an actual direction.

Her boss shot back a terse reply, "Why wait?"

Chapter 7

The next day Madeline read a snippet in *The Boston Globe* about Brooke's murder case, which quoted an unnamed police source as saying "the investigation has stalled, with no suspects identified."

Madeline turned off her computer. The investigation was at a standstill, and here she was, sitting on an old manuscript with a blockbuster motive that at the very least could blow Brooke's murder case wide open. And focus the police attention on Cecil.

No getting around it, doing "nothing" was no longer an option. She had to do something.

But first she needed to be sure that Capote's story about an illegitimate child was true.

Madeline thought about Felix. A man who had, or at least used to have the best sources in Boston. A man who had known everyone in the city. A perfect Plan B had shown up at Coda Gems two days ago, even if he did happen to be an ex-husband. So she'd have to forget feeling bitter, or sad.

Felix would probably find it ironic if she were to ask him for help in what she'd come to hate when they were married—his talent for investigation. Regardless, she should call and ask for his help, although asking for his advice sounded better. Less needy. Yes, that's how she'd phrase it.

Mentioning no names of course, and telling only part of the story. And Felix would be glad to hear from her because after all, reporters, even former reporters, were not like normal people. Their hearts beat for a story.

So Madeline called *The Boston Globe* and asked for Felix Fassbinder.

When he answered she began, "It's Madeline. Do you have a minute?"

"Of course. And good to hear from you Madeline." She had forgotten how his voice sounded on the phone, caring, and sincere. No wonder he'd been good at getting people to open up to him. And that included her.

She said, "Well, I need your...advice. There's something I need to find out that may have happened a long time ago. 'May' being the operative word. It's a long story. Involving, well probably involving organized crime. And I...I would like your opinion. If you have time. I would really, really appreciate it."

"Well you know me," said Felix with a laugh. "I love nothing better than a good story. Especially a long one. And the organized crime part gives it extra juice. How about lunch next week? Towards the end of next week would work. I leave for New York tomorrow for a couple of days."

"The end of next week? Nothing sooner?"

"Sorry, Madeline, but I have deadlines."

She'd heard that one before, about a million times when they'd been married, and she replied, teeth gritted, "Of course, how could I have forgotten? But I thought I'd give it a try. Thanks anyway, and sorry, but I can't wait that long."

Felix said, "I'm sorry too."

Seething, Madeline disconnected.

But he called back an hour later and without preamble said, "Hey Madeline, turns out my conference call at one just cancelled, so I can do lunch. Today. Is that soon enough for you?"

"Today?" she said, but not wanting to sound eager, "Yes, I guess that can work." A pause and she added, "And thank you."

"Great. So noon then, at Abe & Louie's on Boylston Street? Let me check and make sure it's still there." A few seconds later he came back on the line. "It's still there. So I'll see you shortly." And he hung up.

It had seemed odd to thank an ex-husband for making time for lunch, but this was business, not personal. And she did need him.

***

Felix was waiting for her in the lobby of Abe & Louie's when Madeline walked in, his swift glance appraising, like a cop's. He nodded to her cowboy boots, today's a soft, gray leather, "So when did you start channeling Dale Evans?"

"Excuse me, but that would be Annie Oakley, not Dale Evans. There's a big difference. Dale wasn't a real cowgirl," and added dismissively, "she wore skirts. With fringe."

"Of course, what was I thinking?" said Felix as the maître d' welcomed him with a warm smile, saying "It's good to see you again Felix," and showed them to a quiet table in the back. Felix had been a local media celebrity when they'd been married, and everyone seemed to know him. She tensed right before they sat down, hoping the waiter wouldn't ask to take a selfie with the famous Felix Fassbinder. And then the maître did. It wasn't that she hadn't liked sharing Felix.

She had hated it.

Madeline sat down across from Felix, staring at the menu, not looking at him.

They barely spoke that last year of their marriage, he was always on a deadline and she had still been a gem dealer, flying to New York every week. She remembered the last time they'd had lunch together, the day he'd told her he had to be in London for a week, or two. Felix was working on a Russian cybercrime story, one with links to a well-funded Boston tech start-up, and even though he hadn't come out and explicitly said so, one that had some elements of danger.

Four weeks later, still in London, Felix had called, and at the end of an argument about exactly when he'd be coming home, she'd said, her tone bitter, "Look Felix, it's not working, and hasn't for some time, so let's not fool ourselves any longer. Our differences really are irreconcilable and..."

He'd interrupted, "Stop overreacting. Just stop, okay?" Their call lasted for twenty more angry minutes, until she said, "Felix, I want out," and he had hung up. She filed for divorce the next day.

But all that was in the past now.

Madeline watched the waiter set their burgers and fries on the table, and once he left, she began her Mafia story, leaving out names, keeping her motivation vague. Felix had been a reporter after all, and she didn't want him to know more than was necessary. Writers tended to write about what they knew. Look at Truman Capote.

"All quite interesting," Felix said, his tone friendly. "Although you've left some things out. Like any details. Tell me again why you're involved?"

"Because I owe it to someone to find out the truth."

"A friend?"

Madeline hesitated and said, "Yes, a friend. I need to know if this married woman had an affair with a mobster named Benedict. And if she had his child and passed it off as her husband's."

"What was Benedict's last name?"

"I don't know. I'm not even sure that is his first name."

"Well that's hardly helpful. But he was from Boston?"

"Yes, I'm pretty sure he was."

Felix threw his hands up in the air. "You're a little slim on facts you know. So why in God's name are you involved in this?"

"Like I said, I owe someone."

Felix's eyes sharpened, "Still not good enough. Be specific."

"Alright then, if the story is true and there was a child, it's possibly a motive for a crime. An unsolved murder. But before I can go to the police, I need to know if the woman's child was actually fathered not by her husband, but by someone in the Mob. About forty-five or so years ago. The woman," Madeline added, "was from a Boston Brahmin family. That part I know for sure."

Felix said, "Still not enough. All you have is a melodramatic story about an upper-class Boston woman who slept with a Mafia guy years ago and had his child. The Mafia? You're serious?"

"I am. And yes, the Mafia. I just need to know if the story is true. That's why I need your advice."

"You want my advice? Fine, I'll give you my advice. Drop the whole thing. Stay out of it. Stay away." He looked her in the eye, his face grim.

Madeline fumed. Why was he being so difficult? "All right, I don't want your advice. What I want is your help. It's complicated, but I'm already quite involved. And I have to know if the story is true. I will be grateful for anything you can find out. It's important. Seriously."

Felix shook his head and leaned back in his chair, He closed his eyes and Madeline watched him in the silence until finally his blue eyes flashed open and he said, "Well, those were different times then. The Dons tended to be old-fashioned, and they all cheated on their wives of course, but stayed married. And frowned on scandal." He leaned forward. "Forty-five years ago, though. That's tough. I don't know if I can..."

"Felix, you know people who know people. A lot of people."

He sat for a minute, thinking. "Well, you do realize this is close to impossible?"

Madeline nodded, and waited. "You told me once, a long time ago, about your best source. You said you found him in the 'Source Store'. What did you mean?"

He laughed, and checked his cell phone before he said, "You remember the oddest things. I meant other reporters at *The Globe*. We shared sources from time to time. Anyway, the good news is that Whitey Bulger's trial is still sort of recent history. Lots of old Mafia guys surfaced at that circus of a trial. Not sure if I'll find anything though for you through my old sources. It's a crap shoot, but yes, I'll see what I can do for you."

She smiled, "Felix that would be wonderful."

Madeline knew there would be strings attached. Felix had always been a believer in quid pro quo. There was no such thing as free information.

Felix cautioned, "By the way, Madeline, should you be poking around in a Mafia murder case, if that's what this is? You never know who, or what could come crawling out of the woodwork."

"The Mafia is pretty much toothless these days. I'll be careful. I just need to get some facts confirmed."

Felix shook his head and sat back, staring at her. "First of all, Madeline, the Mafia is hardly toothless, a bit hamstrung, but not toothless." A sigh, and then, "At the very least, can you get me the year this bastard was born? Using that term in the literal sense of the word."

"Of course," she said, pulled out her cell phone and googled Cecil Sears.

She looked up. "He was born in 1971."

Felix sighed. "Well, that helps. A little bit. What else do you know about the Mafia guy?"

"I only know that Benedict, if that is his name, ran a drug-smuggling operation, flying drugs in from Miami. And he played the saxophone, and was handsome. And he didn't get along with his father, who was the 'don' or something like that of a Mafia family, in Boston or somewhere on the East Coast. Could have been Boston, or Providence. Or New York. Maybe even Philadelphia. At least I'm pretty sure it was the East Coast."

"Well you have to know that's not all that helpful." Felix glanced at the big pink sapphire ring on her left hand, and his eyes shot up to her face. He said, casually, "That's quite a rock you've got there. Did you get re-married?"

"Not yet."

He looked away, and then back. "I was just curious. Anyway, how is business at Coda Gems?"

"All is well. Business is not booming, but about to boom."

"Must be if you're selling Cartier and Tiffany pearls."

After lunch they had coffee, talking about their old neighborhood in Harvard Square, like two old friends catching up. Except they weren't friends. Which Madeline was about to point out, but didn't. After all, the lunch was going better than she expected, and Felix was on her side. More or less.

After coffee, he signaled for the check."I'll see what I can come up with for you." He glanced at his watch, "Give me your cell phone number and I'll call you once I have something."

Which was so like Felix. Not *if* he had something he'd call her, but *when* he had something.

They left the restaurant and he kissed her goodbye on the cheek and sauntered down the sidewalk. But a saunter with a limp. That was new. She watched him until he disappeared down Boylston Street.

She was glad Felix was back in Boston, if it meant he could help her.

***

When she walked in the door of Coda Gems after lunch the phone was ringing, and Abby answered it and handed it to Madeline. "It's for you."

"Hello, this is Madeline."

"Detective Amick. Can you come down to headquarters this afternoon? At three? I have a couple more questions. It's important."

"Yes, I guess I can be there. What kind of questions?"

"Just follow-up questions."

Madeline hung up and turned to Abby, "That was the detective in charge of Brooke's murder investigation. She has more questions."

"Oh. I would have thought you'd already told her everything you know."

"Obviously not." Madeline sighed.

"Does this have anything to do with that damn manuscript? Or your theory about Cecil murdering his own mother? For God's sake I hope you haven't told the police you think Cecil murdered Brooke?"

"No, I haven't. The detective is probably just being thorough. But I will ask her why the police are following me."

Abby's eyes flashed in surprise. "What? The police are following you?"

"Yes. It's been going on since Brooke was murdered."

"The police have been following you since then? Really Madeline? You should have told me. Following you?"

"I could be mistaken. Maybe I'm just being paranoid." Madeline laughed, "I'm seeing her this afternoon at three. If you don't hear from me by four it's because I'm in jail. Or something."

"That's not funny, Madeline. This is serious."

"You're right. But I'm sure it's nothing."

"If it was nothing, she could have asked you on the phone."

Madeline thought the same thing but that didn't matter now. She'd know soon enough. Maybe she should have a lawyer? But that was for prime suspects, so no, she didn't need a lawyer.

***

Madeline arrived at Boston Police headquarters ten minutes early for her appointment, and gave her name to the officer on duty. She didn't take a seat, but stood by the front desk and only had to wait a minute before Detective Amick walked up. The officer again directed her through the set of scanners in front of the bank of elevators.

On the second floor the detective opened a door midway down the hall and motioned Madeline inside. A different interview room this time but everything else was the same; small, no windows, and tacky furniture.

The detective took a file folder out of her computer bag and said, "So we've talked several times about Mrs. Sears's murder, and you have given us useful information, which I appreciate." A smile. The first ever. Which oddly made Madeline nervous. The detective continued, "But subsequent findings have meant that I do have to follow up more thoroughly. I'm sure you understand."

"Of course I am happy to provide more information. I will do anything I can to be helpful." And then she asked, "But what do you mean, 'subsequent findings'?"

Detective Amick smiled again, which made Madeline even more nervous. The officer said, "All I am looking for is the truth. Who do you think might have wanted to murder Mrs. Sears?"

"Who? I have no idea. I thought a burglar shot Brooke. For her jewelry." Madeline was about to bring up Brooke's family again, Cecil in particular, but changed her mind.

The detective swiveled in her chair. "Maybe burglary was the motive. Or maybe we were meant to think that was the reason she was murdered. Possibly there was another reason." The detective changed the subject. "You knew Brooke quite well. From what I've learned of her, she could be very demanding."

"Demanding? Yes. But I was used to it. She...had her ways."

"She spent a lot of money with your company, didn't she?" The detective looked down at her file. "It would appear she spent a significant amount at your jewelry store in the last two years."

Madeline hesitated, thinking quickly. "She did. I already told you she was a very good customer."

Another smile from the detective, none of them the friendly kind. "And you hoped that would continue, didn't you?"

"It assumed it would continue, at some level. She liked jewelry. Pearl jewelry."

"But when Brooke told you she was no longer interested in buying jewelry, but wanted to focus on writing her book, that must have been a disappointment. I would think it would have been."

"Brooke did say she wanted to focus on her book, but not that we were ending our business relationship. She asked me to work with her on her memoirs, and I said I'd be happy to." The 'happy' part was not quite true, but after all Madeline was being questioned by a homicide detective, so it was close enough.

The detective closed the file. "But Brooke was an extraordinarily important customer of yours, wasn't she? And rich customers do come and go. Happens all the time. I'm aware that you needed to move to a new location. Moving any business is expensive isn't it? Even though it is a necessary one in your case."

Where was the detective getting her information? Madeline didn't like the direction of this conversation, and she said, cautious now, "Well, yes, my partner and I had plans for our business. All small business owners have plans. Tell me again, why did you want to see me today?"

The detective put her hands palms down on her desk, looking at Madeline. "To be honest, your name keeps popping up in my investigation, including the fact that Mrs. Sears left you a significant bequest in her will. Very significant. So I am checking to see if you've told me everything. Have you left anything out? Maybe thinking it's not all that important?"

Madeline leaned forward, and said, her words clipped, "First of all I had no idea Brooke would leave me her pearls, she never said a word about it, not a single word. And when I heard about it, at the lawyer's office, well I was astonished. It came out of the blue."

"I see. Well, that was quite a big bequest that just dropped in your lap. You might have guessed perhaps? Maybe you were able to put two-and-two together beforehand?" The detective arched her eyebrows, waiting for Madeline to say something, but Madeline just stared at her.

Detective Amick continued. "So maybe you went to see Brooke the night she was murdered? To talk about...I don't know, to talk about her book maybe?"

"I already told you, I was home all night. Watching a movie. And I had a pizza delivered. You can check with Amazon, and Papa John's in South Boston, because ..."

"I already have. You bought the movie, you didn't stream it. And the pizza was delivered at 7:05 pm. You could have left by a door in the garage, the one without a camera, and, taken a cab to Beacon Hill. Or gotten a ride with a friend. Of course Brooke would have let you into her townhouse that night. She trusted you. I understand that you would have felt desperate at the thought of losing your best customer. You must have had some inclination that she had changed her will. To your benefit."

Madeline stood up from her chair. "This is ridiculous. First of all, I was not desperate, and second, I did not kill Brooke. I would never have harmed her. Ever. And lastly, if you want to talk to me again, I'll have a lawyer with me. Goodbye."

In a daze, she started to walk out, then turned back. "By the way, your cops are not very good at surveillance. They're pretty easy to spot and I'm tired of them following me around. They are wasting their time."

She strode to the lobby and out the door to the parking lot. Well that interview was a total disaster. Yes, she did need a lawyer, but what she really needed was to get the police on Cecil's trail right away. The question was how.

***

Twenty minutes later Madeline walked in the store and Abby came up to her, brow furrowed. "So how did it go? You look worried.

"I answered more questions, and that was about it." And Madeline shrugged. "It was all just going over the same ground. Routine."

Hardly routine, still she didn't want to alarm Abby. But if she wanted to get the detective's ridiculous focus off her, and onto Cecil, where it belonged, she needed to know more about Brooke's past. Felix had said he would help with the Mafia angle, but who knew how long that would take? And John Althorp was a washout. So how else she could find out if Capote's story was true? She definitely couldn't ask Paige. Which left only Alfred. Of course she should talk to Alfred. After all, he had known Brooke for over thirty years. Yes, that could work. And Detective Amick would have to listen to an esteemed, venerable lawyer, who was an officer of the court after all.

A customer walked in and after Abby went out front, Madeline picked up the phone and called Alfred.

"Alfred, I was wondering if you have time to see me? It's important. I have something I want to show you. It's about Brooke's murder, and I need your opinion."

"My opinion? You should be talking to the police about this, not me."

"Well, I can't, for a couple of reasons. But I do think you'll want to see what I have."

"And it's related to Brooke's murder?"

"Yes."

"Fine then. I can see you day after tomorrow at…"

"Like I said, it's important. Tonight. Can I see you tonight?"

A sigh and then, "Tonight?"

"Yes. Right away. I need to talk to you right away."

Another sigh, and Alfred said, "Fine then. Six thirty, at my office. I can see you for fifteen minutes."

"Great. Thank you."

A minute later Abby walked into the back office, a smile on her face. "I just sold one of Brooke's brooches, the pearl and diamond one. For $29,000."

Madeline walked over and gave her a high five. "You did? You really did? Good God Abby, you are incredible."

"Thanks Madeline. But I'm concerned the police still want to talk to you. I think you should get a lawyer. She, or he, can tell them to go jump in a lake or something."

This time Madeline agreed with her. "Fine then, I will. Tomorrow."

An hour later she and Abby moved the jewelry pieces into the safe and closed up. After Abby said goodbye and left for the night, Madeline stuffed Capote's manuscript in her briefcase. She didn't want to show it to Alfred, but she knew she'd have to, if she wanted his help.

***

Thirty minutes later Madeline sat in Alfred's office, watching as he studied Capote's manuscript, reading the chapter on Brooke for the third time now. Going slow. As Madeline had cautioned, he flipped the pages with the end of a pencil.

He had already agreed to keep their conversation in strictest confidence, and not to mention their conversation to anyone. "And I do mean anyone," she repeated.

Although she did trust him. After all, Brooke had trusted him for thirty years.

Looking up, Alfred finally said, "You say you found this manuscript at Brooke's?"

Madeline thought 'found' sounded better than 'swiped', so she'd gone with that. Yes. Like I said, Brooke told me she wanted to write a book about her life in New York. And she did keep boxes and boxes of papers from those days. Although obviously she wouldn't have included anything from *that* chapter," and Madeline nodded to Capote's manuscript.""

Alfred glanced at her and took off his glasses, rubbing his eyes. "I should think not. Brooke had mentioned to me the day before she was killed that she'd decided to write a book about the people she'd known in New York. She couldn't stop talking about it."

Madeline shrugged and leaned forward. "Do you think the woman in that story is Brooke? And that she had a child by this man Benedict?"

He ignored her questions but asked, his lips pursed, "And you believe Cecil read this chapter, 'A Brahmin Slut'?" Alfred winced when he said the title.

"Yes, I do. He told me there was an old, thick envelope on his mother's desk when he'd stopped by her place after lunch, the day she died. But Brooke must have moved it after he left. I do know Cecil was angry that he couldn't find it. Very angry. Frantic even. He thought I had it. But like I said, I found it later. Anyway, I've read the whole manuscript a couple of times, and this chapter is the only one, that if true, would make Cecil frantic as well as angry."

There was a moment of silence. Alfred sighed again, and flipped to the title page. "Have you read other books by Capote?"

"Years ago."

He said, picking his words, "And do you believe this is authentic? That this is Truman Capote's work?"

"Yes, I think there's a good chance."

Alfred nodded. "As to whether or not the story of an illegitimate child while Brooke was married to Henry is true, just remember that I represent both Cecil and Paige, so I can't really make any further comment."

Madeline said, "But I have to know if the story is true."

He nodded to the manuscript and said, "Thank you for bringing this to me. I have no more to say at this time."

He sat back, studying her, drumming his fingers on the desk. "Have you shown this to the police?"

"No, but only because it's not evidence. But if I know if the story about Brooke is true, about her having an illegitimate child, well then that could possibly be a motive for..."

Alfred put up a hand. "Say no more. I am aware of the implications. Quite aware. Let me think about this. Can you leave this manuscript with me? For three or four days?"

Madeline reached across his desk and slid the manuscript back into the aged manila envelope. "No, I wouldn't be comfortable with that."

Alfred asked her, "Are you keeping it someplace safe?"

"Yes, I am." Another silence. In her experience lawyers always avoided volunteering information, so she continued, "You realize this manuscript gives Cecil a couple of motives for murder? We can't let him get away with..."

Alfred interrupted again, "I said I will get back to you. I need to think about this new information."

Madeline snapped open her briefcase, the click loud in the silence and dropped the bulky envelope inside.

He said, "I'll call you."

She cautioned again, "You'll mention our meeting to no one? Especially..."

Alfred held up his hand again.

Madeline continued, "And the manuscript, you must not tell anyone that I have it."

"Like I said, I will not mention this manuscript or our conversation to anyone. Thank you for bringing this to my attention."

They shook hands but when Madeline got to the door, she looked back. He was staring out the window at the swans swimming on the pond, and then he turned toward her, his face dull-red with rage.

So Alfred believed the story was true. Possibly even that Cecil had murdered Brooke. At last she was getting somewhere.

***

The next afternoon Cecil sat in his home office, looking at his watch every few minutes. Waiting for Alfred. Cecil had just spent two days in Washington, meeting with members of the Judiciary Committee, necessary of course, but time consuming. Which meant he was behind in his trial prep work, so he had a full day's work ahead. On a Saturday. However, Alfred had been quite insistent that he needed to see him. Today. About Paige.

He heard the doorbell ring, and then his wife showed Alfred into Cecil's office.

Alfred began, "So I have researched recent case law and there's been nothing new about circumventing the 'Spend Thrift' clause in your father's trust documents. Which means I am not able to give Paige any kind of advance whatsoever."

For the next twenty minutes the two lawyers talked about the clause, which barred trust beneficiaries from borrowing against future dividends.

Cecil finally said, "So there are no loop holes? No way to get around it? There is absolutely no way you can give her an advance?"

"That is correct, since an advance is basically a loan. I'm sure your father meant the clause as a protection against potential creditors. Regardless, Paige cannot legally access any funds prior to the distribution date. I am sorry."

Cecil glanced at his watch. Surely this was a conversation they could have had over the phone? "Well Alfred, thank you for checking into this."

But Alfred didn't stand up. Instead he said, "There's something else. Years ago I remember she had an old manuscript, written by a famous writer, I forget his name. It was in a stack of papers I was reviewing for her. I'm sure it had ended up in the pile accidentally."

Cecil hid his unease, and said, guarded now, "My mother was a bit of pack rat wasn't she? I think I remember the manuscript you're talking about. Quite thick, and rather beaten up?" Alfred nodded, and Cecil watched him. So what was the old man getting at? "As I remember, when I mentioned it she told me a friend of hers had written it as a prank, and she thought it was quite funny." Cecil didn't take his eyes off Alfred. "Do you happen to know where it is? I'm gathering together all of Mother's old papers, but I haven't come across it."

Alfred took off his glasses, rubbing his eyes. "I have no idea where it is. Funny though, I was just thinking about it the other day. I only read parts of it years ago...there was something in it about an illegitimate child. An interesting story, and I always wondered how it ended. I could never ask her about it of course."

There was a heavy silence and Cecil stood up, "Well, Alfred, if it shows up, I'll send it along for you to take a look at." He laughed. "And you can find out how it ends. Anyway, thank you again for coming in. I will tell Paige that you and I spoke, and there is no way she can get an advance."

Alfred finally stood up and Cecil walked him down the hall to the front door and went back to his office. And with a sigh sat back at his desk. Cecil had no doubt the real reason Alfred wanted to come by was to let him know that he'd read "A Brahmin Slut" in that godforsaken manuscript. And Alfred had probably guessed he was the illegitimate child. So why did he bring it up, and then leave?

Maybe because Alfred meant to let him know he intended to do something about it? Which also could mean he knew where the manuscript was. What did the old lawyer have in mind?

Cecil knew it was much too late in the game to just go ahead and fire Alfred. The man knew far too many secrets for his own good. He'd have to do something about Alfred, as soon as possible. He was half-way through reviewing a deposition when his wife stuck her head in the door.

"Paige is here."

What did she want now? Cecil sighed. "Tell her I'm on a conference call. No wait, send her in."

A minute later Paige strolled in. "Sorry to just drop in. Anyway, I just saw Alfred in the driveway. He said he'd talked to you about the advance, and the old bastard told me it was not legally possible." She pulled out a chair and sat down. "I mean really, what is the use of having a lawyer if they can't figure out a way to bend the rules? Isn't that what law school is all about?"

Cecil didn't rise to the bait. "Alfred and I talked for a long time about the trust language. And I'm sorry."

"Me too. I asked him to double check, and he said it would be a waste of time. We should fire him, I mean now that Mother's dead we—"

"No, this is not a good time to fire him."

"But can't you just get rid of him some other way? He gives me the creeps."

Cecil shrugged, not wanting to have this conversation with Paige. He changed the subject, "So how is your...I think you called it 'location scouting' going?"

"Great actually. Really great. That's why I need $20,000."

Cecil didn't say anything and the seconds ticked by.

Paige leaned toward him, her eyes narrowed. "By the way, that was a request."

"Really? Funny, it didn't sound like one."

"Fine. Can I borrow $20,000...please? I found a perfect location. But Massachusetts is ridiculously expensive. Who do these people think they are?"

He sighed. "Maybe you should do your filming in California?"

"So what do you want me to do next, beg?"

He toyed with his pen, watching her. After a minute she stood up, "Well, thanks for nothing Brother Dear." And with her right hand she shoved the files on his desk to the floor and strode out.

A minute later he heard the front door slam, and then the sound of a car screeching its way down the street.

Cecil should have given Paige a check on the spot, but she was unbearable. He went back to the stack of papers on his desk. He'd send her a check for $20,000. In a couple of days.

***

First thing on Monday, Madeline called their business lawyer, Stan, who was surprised when she asked for the names of the top five criminal attorneys in Boston.

Stan laughed, "You must have a customer who's in a big-time jam."

"Not exactly. I'm the one who's in a big-time jam. I think. The police are giving me a hard time, over nothing."

She told him about her conversations with Detective Amick, and Stan said, not laughing now, that he'd get back to her in half an hour and he did, emailing Madeline a list of five criminal lawyers. All highly credentialed, and all no doubt expensive. Madeline told Abby about the list when she walked in the door at nine.

Abby said, "Well, that's good news. The sooner you have a lawyer the better."

"Yes, I guess so. I'll start calling them when it quiets down."

"It's quiet now," commented Abby.

But it didn't stay that way. Business had definitely picked up since they'd run the ads, and by three they'd sold another pearl necklace from Brooke's collection, and four pieces from their own gold and diamond inventory.

Abby said, after the last customer left, "I didn't want to interrupt when we were so busy. But Christopher from Saks called an hour ago and he has two orchestra seat tickets for opening night of *Der Rosenkavalier* at the Boston Opera House tonight. He wanted to know if you and I wanted them, so I said yes, and we're to pick them up at the box office. Anyway, I thought it would be fun. Especially since we now have another sale of Brooke's pearls to celebrate."

"Celebrate? Yes. To the opera? No. Definitely no. And especially not that one. You go, and take a friend."

But Abby was having none of that. "I want to go, and I want you to come with me. It won't kill you to come, so let's just go. And it is opening night after all."

"But opening night? I don't feel like getting all dressed up and—"

"Well, it can be formal-ish, but for God's sake, Madeline, just come. We deserve a swank night out. May I point out we never do swank? And I have sold four of Brooke's pieces after all and—"

"Alright, I'll go, because yes, you are amazing." She grinned, "And, I'll be happy about it."

Abby laughed. "Well, that's a relief."

Before they closed the store, Madeline took Brooke's big pearl and diamond necklace out of the safe, and dropped the velvet box in her briefcase. After all, opening night at the opera was the perfect place to wear the necklace. Besides, this might be the only chance she'd ever have to wear it, since it could sell any day. But not likely. Still…

When Madeline got home, she flipped through the row of black dresses in her closet, but the best one to wear with the necklace of three strings of pearls and an eleven-carat diamond pendant was the simple, black Versace she'd worn to Brooke's funeral.

Which seemed oddly appropriate.

***

An hour and a half later Madeline and Abby walked into the lobby of the Opera House in downtown Boston, an historic 1920's building with soaring ceilings, marble floors and gilded walls. Crowded with men in black tie and women in varying shades of the same color. Madeline just wanted to get through the night, so alcohol seemed a good idea. She went to the bar and came back with two glasses of champagne, handing one to Abby, who tonight wore a gold lame dress. Madeline had never seen her partner in anything but 100% natural fibers. Gold lame? Abby's dark hair was slicked back, and she even had at least four carats of diamonds on her ear lobes.

"Well, you pulled out all the stops," commented Madeline.

Abby shrugged. "May I say 'ditto'? That necklace suits you."

Madeline laughed, "I had to wear it, at least once. I don't think Brooke ever wore it the entire time I knew her. I'm pretty sure it never left her safe deposit box."

Fifteen minutes later Madeline went back for another glass of champagne, this one just for her, since Abby was pretty much a one-drink woman. When she came back and was talking to Abby about their sales numbers, when a voice said behind her said, "'Of all the gin joints, in all the towns, in all the world...'"

Madeline finished the quote from *Casablanca*, "'... she walks into mine.'" and turned to smile at Felix, black-tie handsome. She was surprised to see him, but then again, she shouldn't have been. Opera was one of his passions that she hadn't shared.

He kissed her on the cheek and in the noisy din of the Opera House foyer she introduced Abby, and Felix introduced the dark-haired woman in a clinging red dress beside him, whose name Madeline didn't catch. Felix and Abby started talking about Strauss, so Madeline tried to strike up a conversation with Felix's date, a model from the Czech Republic. But the woman's English skills were marginal, and she also was an idiot.

Madeline said to her, "I've never seen "Der Rosenkavalier" before. Do you know the story line?"

"Story line?"

"Sorry, I mean do you know what the opera is about?"

"About? Oh. Singing. All sing."

Madeline continued, "The opera is about an older woman in love with a younger man. No surprise, it doesn't end well. At least not for the older woman."

Felix's date laughed, as if Madeline had said something hilarious. Why was Felix with her? Other than the obvious. Then his date said, "Old woman stupid." And laughed again. Madeline turned away.

"So you've become an opera fan?" Felix said to Madeline. "That's a shock. You said once you'd rather perforate an ear drum." He leaned closer, "By the way, you look wonderful tonight, and I like the bling." She didn't say anything and he added, "Well, it's good to see you. Just so you know, I started checking around about your story. And I was told I need to talk to a hot-shot stringer for *The Globe*, but she's out of the country, so it may take awhile. I'll call you."

Nodding to her and Abby, Felix took his date's arm and they walked over to the bar.

Madeline said to Abby, "By the way, that's my ex-husband. He's back in Boston."

"Oh my God, that's him?" said Abby, staring after Felix. "You're kidding? I thought he was in Chicago, or somewhere in the Midwest. What's he doing in Boston?"

"He's back at *The Globe* again."

"Oh. Well, you seem on good terms. I thought you hated him."

"I don't hate Felix; I was just done with him. But he is helping me out with something, so I have to be gracious."

Abby laughed. "He is quite good-looking."

Madeline shrugged but didn't say anything. What did Felix mean by 'it might take awhile?' She watched him and his date standing at the bar now, the woman throwing back her shimmering brown hair and laughing at everything Felix said, her eyes never leaving his face.

Thank God she'd never been like that.

She watched a tuxedoed man walk up to Felix and the two shook hands. Maybe Felix knew him, maybe he didn't. When they had been married, total strangers often came up to Felix, wanting to talk.

The lights dimmed so she and Abby made their way to their orchestra seats, four rows from the stage, and after a long two hours the fat lady finally sang. As Madeline filed out of the Opera House with Abby, she looked around for Felix and his date in her too-tight dress, but didn't see them.

And was annoyed with herself that she'd even looked for him.

***

First thing the next morning Madeline called Felix at *The Globe* and left a message. He called her back five minutes later.

He began, "I was surprised to see you last night but...never mind. So what did you think of 'Der Rosenkavalier'?"

Madeline said, "It was good," and left it at that. Opera was something one had to gain an appreciation of when one was young. Like smoking. Madeline continued, "So I thought I'd check, and see how long you think 'awhile' might be. The Mafia thing you know. You said it might be awhile."

"Well, that's hard to say. The woman I need to talk to is somewhere in Pakistan right now on a story, and nobody knows for sure when she'll be back. Could be a week, could be a month. The good news is I've been told she's a walking encyclopedia on New England crime families. I got the impression that if that was a category on Jeopardy she'd win, hands down."

"It could be a month?"

"Yes. So you'll just have to be patient."

Madeline decided she didn't have to be anything and said, "Well, thanks for checking into this. Really, thank you." And hung up. The thought of twiddling her thumbs for a month while Cecil was still walking around not only free but also not under investigation was unbearable. Madeline went back to her stack of gem appraisals.

Abby walked in then and said, "I think I just saw Cecil out front, sitting in a black Porsche across the street. I don't think he saw me, he was busy staring at the front door of the building. But maybe it wasn't him. Anyway, I came in the back way. Just in case."

Madeline froze. If it was Cecil, why was he outside? So maybe he had watched Brooke's security camera file the night she'd grabbed the manuscript. She glanced at their safe. Did he know she had it? Madeline said, "If he shows up, I'll call the cops."

Abby opened a drawer, pulled out a sleek Sig Sauer and set it on top of her desk, barrel facing the wall. "I've been meaning to mention I have this. Just in case."

Madeline took a step back. "A gun? You've got a gun? Here? I never saw it before. Ever. What in the…"

"My father gave it to me when I graduated from college. He…well, I grew up in the Midwest, and the Second Amendment is pretty big there, you know. Anyway, I've had it ever since. At home." and she laughed. "But after Brooke was murdered, I thought it might be better to have it here, in case we became a target or something. And yes, I do know how to shoot, and yes, I am licensed. Have been since I was twenty-one." She looked out to the front door and back to Madeline, "Because you never know who might show up."

Madeline stared at her conservative business partner. Predictable, quiet Abby. Who was decidedly more of an Annie Oakley than she was. Madeline looked at the gun. "Is it loaded?"

Abby laughed, "Of course it's loaded."

"And you say you have a license?"

"Ditto."

A ridiculous question. Abby would never break the law.

Madeline said, "Shouldn't it be locked up or something, not just lying around in a drawer? Maybe it should be in our safe?"

Abby stared at her. "And what am I supposed to do if a thug shows up? Say, 'Hold on just a second while I unlock the safe and pull out my weapon?'"

"Good point." Madeline couldn't take her eyes off Abby's gun. "You know, I've decided I should learn how to shoot. Can I…can I hold your gun…just to see how it feels?"

"No. Not unless you take a gun safety class first. The safety catch is on, but I don't want you to accidentally shoot yourself. Or me."

"Don't worry. I'll just use it to shoot Cecil."

"That's not funny," Abby sighed and put the gun back in the bottom drawer. "I'll do the shooting here."

"Are you a good shot?"

"Yes," said Abby. "Yes, I am."

Madeline wasn't sure if she was relieved or alarmed that her business partner was armed. She said to Abby, "And you really think Cecil was parked out front?"

"I said I couldn't be sure. But I thought it was him. I'm pretty sure it was him."

"Well, at least we're prepared."

Abby just gave her a look, and walked out to the front.

Madeline went back to her gem appraisals. Couldn't Cecil ask the police to get a search warrant and have them show up at the store and demand she open the safe? She googled 'search warrant' and realized that scenario was unlikely. Regardless, she needed to hire an attorney, so Madeline spent the next hour at the store calling the five criminal lawyers on Stan's list and was able to get immediate appointments with two.

Once she decided on a lawyer, all she'd need to do was write out a check for a retainer, likely a big one, and bingo, she'd have a lawyer. But she worried about Cecil. If it was Cecil sitting in a car outside.

***

As Madeline drove home that night, she focused on a dark car just behind her that made every turn she did. Whoever was following her wasn't making much of an effort to be unnoticed. She made two left-hand turns just to check, but the dark car was still behind. So Madeline got on the expressway and was able to shake off the tail with three hair-raising lane changes, followed up with an abrupt exit out of the scrum of rush-hour traffic. Whoever had been tailing her had been sloppy, so maybe it wasn't the police? Maybe it had been Cecil.

Once she was home, she double-checked the dead bolt on both her front and back doors. Maybe she should call Detective Amick? No, she decided, she needed to stay far away from that woman, who seemed anxious to arrest her for something. Too bad she didn't have a gun.

Madeline fell asleep in the living room later that night watching a cop show on TV. At two in the morning she dragged herself off to bed. Her own life had more drama than any cop show.

Chapter 8

By the end of the next day, Madeline had her very own criminal defense attorney, Anthony, confident, smart, and perceptive. He listened to her story and after almost an hour meeting in his office told her, "Well, the police clearly don't have any evidence, but if they get in touch with you again, call me immediately. You are not to talk to them without me."

She did feel better having a lawyer, but still was on edge, wondering if Detective Amick, or Cecil would show up at the store any minute, but neither came bursting in.

Then on Friday Abby answered the phone and handed it to Madeline.

It was Felix. "So I have some good news," he began. "Susan, the *Globe* stringer I mentioned? The one who knows about the Mafia? She got back from Pakistan early."

"Early? She's back early? That is great news."

"I guess so, although maybe not for her, since I gather she was kicked out of the country. Anyway, I talked to her yesterday, and by the way, I had to promise all kinds of favors to get her help, so you owe me double. I told her the specifics of the Mafia gossip I'm looking for, and said it was urgent."

There was a long silence. Madeline prompted, "And?"

"Susan called me at home late last night. She went to Providence right after we talked to see an old Mob guy she knows. Apparently quite well. She didn't want to give me any particulars, or names of course."

A silence. Why was Felix dragging this out? "Madeline said, "Well, that's great. And…"

"I'm not sure how great it is. You know, I don't think you should be involved in this, Madeline. These people are dangerous."

"I'm already involved in it. Up to my neck so to speak. So what did she say for God's sake?"

A long sigh from Felix and then he said, "So, yes, there was a son of a Mafia don in Boston who supposedly had an illegitimate child in the 1970's – when that was still scandalous. And yes, the mother was a married woman from a prominent New England family."

Madeline smiled. So Capote's story about Brooke was true! Possibly true anyway. She said, "That's incredible. You are a wonder. But I need to know more. You do know more, don't you? Did she find out the woman's name? I just need to be sure you're on the right track."

"I asked Susan, but the man didn't know. And you're involved in this again because …why?"

"Because it's possibly a motive for murder. But Felix, I do need to know more. And like you said, you do owe me."

Felix laughed, "Madeline, I never said that. What I did say was that I was sorry."

"Same thing. But can we meet for just a couple of minutes right away? Not long, I promise. Over a cup of coffee?" She wasn't going to beg, then changed her mind. "Please Felix? I am desperate for more information. Truly, deeply." In the early days of their marriage she used to tell him, 'I love you truly, deeply.' He wouldn't have forgotten her words. Still, as soon as she said it she wished she could take them back.

A pause, then Felix said, "Fine then, let's meet. I'll see you in an hour at the Café Nero, on Washington St. It's…"

"I know where it is. I really appreciate this," and hung up, a smile on her face. A grim smile. She was really getting somewhere. It was about time.

***

An hour later she and Felix were sitting at a back table in the café. He'd kissed her on the cheek when she walked in, so obviously they were now firmly in the amicable, kiss-on-the-cheek phase of their divorced life. Like Charles and Diana in the mid-90's, but without the royal children. Or Diana's $25 million dollar divorce settlement. Except Madeline wasn't feeling especially amicable that morning. She should have left Felix two years into their marriage, not four.

She put down the menu and studied him, and Felix, glancing up said, "What are you looking at?"

"Oh, nothing."

After the waiter walked away with their order Felix began, "Well, it seems as if you might have stepped in a hornet's nest."

Madeline said, "I have?"

"You have." He stopped. "You know this whole thing is a bad idea. Fascinating actually, but bad. People can…get into trouble for knowing too much you know."

Madeline stared at him. So now he was worried? She said, "Come on Felix you have to tell me what you know. You know you have to."

He looked at her, annoyed. "Actually, I don't have to. But I will. But first, tell me what you will do with this information. I have to protect Susan, because…"

"She is a source, and sources are your lifeblood," interrupted Madeline. "I know. You told me that a hundred times. I just need to know if the story I told you was true. That's all I need to know."

"Fine then. It's true. Or rather it looks like it's true. Are you happy now?" He picked up the menu.

Madeline glared at him. "Alright Felix, I lied. I do want the details. Not that I'll tell anyone of course. It will just be between you and me. It won't kill you to give me details. Since you know."

Felix winced and leaned toward her, his voice cautious. "I can't believe I let you talk me into this."

"To be honest, it wasn't that hard."

He stared at the menu for a full minute, his jaw clenched, then looked up and said, his voice flat. "Have you ever heard of the Barzetti crime family?"

Madeline shook her head, and pulled her iPad out of her purse, clicking it on. "No, I never heard of them. How do you spell Barzetti?"

He nodded to her iPad. "Put that away, there can't be a record of this conversation, so just listen. The Barzetti's were a small, but lethal organization in Boston years ago. Lucca Barzetti was the head of it in the 60's and early 70's, and ran the usual drugs and gambling syndicates."

"I never heard the name. Until now."

"Whatever. Lucca had two sons, and the oldest was named Ben. "

"That's perfect," said Madeline. So the names more or less matched. In Capote's story, the name of Brooke's lover was Benedict.

Felix asked, "What's perfect?"

"Sorry. Never mind. Continue. Please."

"Anyway, Ben, the son didn't get along with his father, who was very Old-School Mafia, and this Ben hated the Family business and wanted out. But his old man wouldn't let him. And here is where it gets really interesting, from your perspective anyway. Ben supposedly had a girlfriend from Boston, a blue-blood Yankee. Who was married. And Ben got her pregnant."

He paused and Madeline, barely breathing, watched him, not moving.

Felix continued, "So the guy's father, Lucca got wind of this affair and the pregnancy, and told Ben to drop her immediately. Anyway, according to Susan, the two got into an ugly argument at a restaurant in the North End and Lucca threatened to have the woman "disposed of," and then Ben stood up and slugged his father, and knocked him unconscious. Someone called an ambulance and Lucca ended up in the hospital with a broken jaw and a concussion." Felix stopped.

"And...?" said Madeline.

"There was, according to Susan, another big argument three days later, and Lucca threatened again to have Ben's lover murdered. So Ben went to the FBI, and turned informant on his old man and his Mafia activities. And the Feds got enough evidence to indict Lucca on RICO charges."

"Just curious, but how?"

"The FBI had Ben wear a wire, and they ended up with a list of names and dates, and they arrested Lucca and he was put on trial. And based on the evidence, Lucca knew it was his son Ben who had cooperated with the Feds.

Anyway, Lucca was found guilty, and sentenced to twenty years. And then Ben was shot dead in downtown Boston a week later, during rush hour, by Davio, his younger brother. On orders from Lucca."

Madeline looked up, her eyes wide, as Felix continued, "At least that's what Susan was told. Anyway, the police never solved the murder, so Davio got away scot-free. Although since Ben was also the primary suspect in a cold-case murder of an undercover cop the year before, maybe the Boston police weren't knocking themselves out to solve his murder."

So Capote's story was true! She said, "Felix, this is unbelievable. But how twisted. So what happened to the woman and her child?"

Felix shook his head. "Susan said her source didn't know. He didn't even know the woman's name. The guy told Susan it was all just an old story he'd heard years ago." He looked at Madeline, "Anyway, Susan told me that Davio, the brother, did try and find out who the woman was, and where she lived, and have her and the child killed. But he wasn't able to find the woman. No one knew anything about her, except that she was rich, beautiful, and married, and had a child.

"Anyway," Felix continued, "Lucca never made it out of prison, but died there, five years into his twenty-year sentence. And then, about two years after Lucca died, Davio folded up the family syndicate in Boston and moved to Las Vegas. And that's all the information I have. End of story."

"But there's more? Surely there's more?"

"Isn't that enough?"

"Come on Felix, there has to be more to this. Surely you have some ideas?"

"Look Madeline, I don't like this digging around in old Mob stories. I said I'd try and help you, and I did. So now you know."

Madeline said, "Fine then. Thank you for this information, really, thank you. You know what I think? I think Davio, who must be in his seventies now, maybe this Davio decided to make one last effort to find this woman and have her murdered before he died. After all, you did say they were a bloodthirsty family. But this time he finally found her. And had her murdered."

Felix looked at her, not moving. All he said was, "You watch too much TV."

"You know, this sounds like a gangster movie."

Felix shrugged, "Well, it is true that Mafia families like the Barzetti's never forget. Fifty years ago or yesterday, it's all the same thing to them."

Madeline said, "So you do believe that I'm right?"

"Well, let's just say that it is a possibility. And, now that I think about it, if I were the woman's son, I'd be pretty nervous right now. You know you've never given me any names in your story. Why not?"

Madeline said, "Because I don't want to. Not yet. But I find it hard to believe that old vendettas still exist."

Felix said, "You're naïve if you don't. Mafia families change and morph into new criminal enterprises, but loyalty is the glue for all criminal gangs." Felix continued, "You know Madeline I don't like this at all. It's a bad idea for you to be in the middle of this. I didn't come back to Boston for…"

She interrupted. "Well Felix, I'm not really in the middle of it. I'm just sort of on the periphery. A long ago periphery." Madeline signaled the waiter for the check.

"But you just told me earlier you were in it up to your neck. So which is it?"

"Actually, all of the above."

He shrugged, "I dug up this information only because you asked me to, because you said it was important. But you're withholding information."

"I have to. Trust me."

"Well, it's too bad you don't trust me. Why are you shielding this woman? Who is she?"

She handed the waiter her credit card and ignored his questions. "Felix I really appreciate this information. You are wonderful. I'll take you out to dinner soon, as a thank you. An expensive dinner." They walked out of the restaurant and after the now standard kiss on the cheek from Felix she set off back to the store. Finally, she had real, or likely real validation of who murdered Brooke.

And big surprise, it looked like it wasn't Cecil.

She took a deep breath. She was off the hook now, so to speak. She'd done what she needed to do for Brooke. She could well and truly back away.So Cecil hadn't murdered her, which meant she could now leave catching her killer totally up to the police.

Except, if she didn't continue to follow up on Brooke's murder, then it was likely her killer would get away with murder. The cops wouldn't pick up the Mob connection on their own —how could they? Since they didn't know the whole story. Which meant Madeline couldn't quit now, almost, but not quite yet.

What she had to do next was figure out the best way to turn the steely eyes of Detective Amick off her, to where she now knew they really belonged. On the Mafia. Madeline knew she was in way over her head. But she was almost done.

***

On her way home that evening Madeline wished she hadn't told Felix she'd take him out to dinner. She didn't want to be friends with her ex. Still, she'd said she would, so she'd have to. She'd pick a place that wasn't romantic.

When she walked in the store the next morning Abby was showing a woman in a beige suit, beige heels and beige silk scarf one of Brooke's smaller pearl necklaces, as well as the big necklace with the diamond pendant. Madeline guessed the woman must be from one of Boston's upscale suburbs. Or, maybe she was from Connecticut, where women lived in beige, not like New Yorkers who mostly dressed in black. Like her.

Still, she couldn't concentrate on work. She had googled the Barzetti family right after meeting Felix for coffee. And yes, like he had said, Lucca Barzetti had been sentenced to prison for 20 years, and had died there, but there was no information about his sons.

Regardless, she was definitely onto something. Not at all what she expected, but definitely something. Which meant she could now take Capote's manuscript to Detective Amick, and be done with Brooke's murder investigation.

Abby left the store shortly after to meet with Lynne, the real estate broker to look at more potential retail spaces on Newbury Street, and during the mid-afternoon lull Madeline pulled out Capote's manuscript, and re-read the chapter on Brooke and her lover, with the ending vague. Truman had written that the man had been murdered "to settle an old Family score." Which she now knew meant Ben was murdered because he got his father sent to prison. Made sense, in a Mafia sort of way. What Truman didn't write, if Felix's source was correct, was that Benedict, although Madeline now knew his real name was Ben, had been murdered by his own brother. Truman had written that he'd been shot dead by a man named Kane, a member of the crime family. Which was likely Capote's heavy-handed joke on the Cain and Abel story? Still everything fit with what Felix had told her. Which meant the chapter, "A Brahmin Slut," in typical Capote fashion, was more or less true.

So it was very possible that this Davio Barzetti had put out a Mafia 'hit' on Brooke, even after all these years. And now that Madeline thought about it, hadn't one of the newspapers said Brooke had been murdered 'execution style'? That sounded like the Mob to her. She said aloud, "Dear Brooke, what a sad, complicated mess you got yourself into."

Capote knew right where his society friends' vulnerabilities were. And he homed in on them.

And yes, she could 'suggest' to Detective Amick that she look at the Barzetti family, and show her Capote's manuscript and get the police on the right trail. Which was her goal after all wasn't it?

Then Madeline froze. There was another 'but'. A big one, which Felix had mentioned in passing. She couldn't ignore the very real possibility that Cecil might now be in immediate danger. Because if the Mafia had gone after Brooke, they'd be sure to come after him too. Which meant she had to warn Cecil, she had to let him know he might be in danger. Brooke would have wanted her to do that, Brooke would have wanted her to look out for Cecil. And Madeline sighed. So she would have to take care of that first.

But she'd have to warn him carefully. The high and mighty Cecil Sears wouldn't be at all happy to hear from her. At all. She wouldn't show him Capote's manuscript of course. So what could she say? Maybe she'd just tell him that Brooke had mentioned a number of times that she'd had a falling out with the Barzetti family years ago, over what, Madeline didn't know.

Madeline sighed. And then she'd have to tell Cecil that he should ask the police to check into a possible mob connection to his mother's murder. And that he should be careful because they might be coming after him. Even to her the story sounded seriously preposterous.

The good part was if Cecil <u>did</u> suggest to the police there might be a possible Barzetti connection to his mother's murder the Boston Police would have to follow-up. How could they not? He was a Sears, so they'd have to pay attention. All Madeline had to do was get Cecil to think her tale, her wild, cockamamie suggestion of a Mafia link to Brooke's murder just might have some validity. And of course too the fact that he might be in danger.

At best it would be a tricky conversation, but one she would have to have in person. Definitely not over the phone. So she'd call Cecil and set up a meeting and then tell him.

After all, Brooke would never forgive Madeline if she let her son be murdered.

Madeline locked the store's front door and stuck their 'Out to Lunch' sign on it so she wouldn't be interrupted. She paced up and down the store, going over exactly what she'd say to Cecil. Parsing every word. And she jotted down a rough script, and changed it about ten times until it was as good as she could get it. Only then did she go to her desk in the back and call him.

He picked up, "Cecil Sears."

And she began, "It's Madeline Lane, and there's something I need to talk to you about. Not over the phone, but in person. Today. It's about your mother's murder."

Cecil said, "What do you want Madeline? You're involved in my mother's homicide investigation now? This is really too much. If you have information you should just go to the police."

"Sorry, but I need to see you. And talk."

Cecil replied, "You know what Madeline? I can't, I'm busy. I'm busy all day. Don't call me again. Ever," his tone cold, layered with dislike.

She said, "Wait, wait, don't hang up. Don't hang up. This is important, and it shouldn't wait. I need to see you right away."

A pause, and Cecil sighed, "Well, what is it you want to talk about? Exactly?"

"I have information, important information. And I don't want to go into it over the phone. How about if we get together at the bar in the Parker House this afternoon? That's close to your office isn't it? The bar downstairs? Today. I don't think it should wait. And like I said, it involves the Sears's family."

Cecil said, cautious now, "Does this have anything to do with my sister Paige?"

"Paige? No, nothing to do with Paige."

Cecil said, "Oh. It doesn't?" A silence. "And it's critical?"

"Yes, it is."

He sighed, "Fine then. All I can say is this had better be worth my time."

"It will be. Does five o'clock work? I'll explain everything when I see you at the Parker House. In their bar, 'The Last Hurrah'. The one downstairs."

Cecil said, his voice cold, abrupt. "You already told me that. I know where it is. I'll see you at five."

Madeline didn't thank him because he should be thanking her, and she hung up. Relieved, because she knew it was the right thing to do.

Abby walked in ten minutes later, excited about the retail spaces she'd just seen with Lynne, and Madeline did her best to be enthusiastic. The next hours dripped by and at four thirty she jammed a beret on her head because it was windy, and drove to The Parker House.

***

Madeline parked a block away and walked to the hotel, going over again what she'd say to Cecil. She was positive that he'd read Capote's chapter on Brooke, and so he knew the truth about his real father. But she couldn't let him know that she knew. Never that. She'd just tell him that Brooke had mentioned a number of times there was 'bad blood' between the Sears and the Barzetti's over something that had happened a long time ago. And that Brooke was afraid of the Barzetti family. Yes, that sounded good. And no, she had no idea why, but Brooke was definitely afraid of them. And maybe they had her murdered, and, just maybe they would come after him. So Cecil should let the police know. Cecil would accuse her of barging into Brooke's

138

murder investigation, but that was just too bad.

When Madeline walked into the lobby of the Parker House, she heard a siren blaring outside on the street, then two, then a string of them as she went down a flight of stairs to the bar. Which was crowded with men and women in suits, lawyers no doubt, and a sprinkle of tourists in jeans and sweatshirts. She surveyed the room, no Cecil at the bar or at one of the tables. She ordered a Diet Coke and waited, watching the door. More people squeezed into the bar.

After half an hour and no Cecil, she called his cell, but he didn't pick up. So where was he? Madeline walked back up the stairs to the hotel lobby. Maybe he'd misunderstood and was waiting there? But the only people in the lobby were checking in. None of them Cecil.

She glanced outside at Tremont Street, three police cars were parked on the sidewalk, red and blue lights flashing. She walked through the revolving door outside and there was Detective Amick, her hands shoved in the pockets of her coat, talking to a state trooper. Not happy, but then the woman was never happy. The detective was in blue slacks and blue blazer, her dark hair pulled back in a chignon. Almost glamorous, but the glint of handcuffs dangling from her belt spoiled the effect.

She overheard Detective Amick snap at the state trooper, "I have jurisdiction over this homicide, you don't," and the trooper glared and walked away.

Curious, Madeline walked up to her, "A murder? Here? So what happened?"

Detective Amick turned, saw Madeline, and started to walk away. But when Madeline blurted, "The victim wouldn't happen to be Cecil Sears would it?" the detective stopped and whirled around. The dead-stop kind of stop.

"Why do you think Cecil Sears was the victim? Why did you ask me that? What do you know? The victim's name hasn't been released to the public." The detective walked up to Madeline, her drawn face now just inches away, demanding, "Answer my question, why do you think it was Cecil Sears who was just killed? What do you know?"

Madeline stared at the detective. "Oh. Well. That was just a guess. I was supposed to meet him for drinks at the Parker House at five, but he didn't show up and didn't answer his cell phone so I came out to see..." and her voice trailed off.

She didn't like the way Detective Amick was looking at her.

The detective said, "You were to meet Cecil Sears? Here?"

"Yes. At the bar downstairs in The Parker House."

"At what time, and why?"

"I just told you, at five. At the bar. To talk about his mother." Madeline thought quickly and added, "I just wanted to talk to him about Brooke. I got here at five minutes to five, ordered a Diet Coke, and waited."

"Who else knew you were meeting him?"

"No one."

The detective gave her a cop stare, as if she would like nothing better than to clap her handcuffs around Madeline's wrists and yank her off to headquarters. But Detective Amick only warned her, "Don't go anywhere. Don't move. I'll be right back. I need to talk to you," and she went into the lobby of the hotel, Madeline staring after.

Cecil had just been shot and killed? Murdered? She looked at the front door of the hotel. So what was the detective doing inside, checking on her story? Madeline hoped the waiter would remember her. Maybe he'd remember the beret. Still, there was no way Madeline was going to wait around for the detective to come back.

In a daze, she walked back to her car.

She needed to figure out what to do next. She had to do something. Right away.

ACT III

Chapter 9

Madeline started up her car, and drove for a couple of blocks before pulling over in an alley. She sat behind the wheel, thinking. So the Mafia had gotten to Cecil before she could warn him. And now he was dead. Her hands were shaking when she turned on the radio, and she clasped them around the steering wheel until the shaking stopped.

She had been right to want to warn Cecil, but she'd been too late. She picked up her cell phone. She should let Felix know. When he answered, she said in a rush, "I have to see you. Right away. The story I told you about, the woman from Boston and the Mafia? Well, her son was just murdered in downtown Boston. Shot dead. He was on his way to see me."

Felix said, "You're kidding? All right, you're not kidding. And you're okay?"

"Yes."

"And who was just killed? You never did give me any names. I do need to know. Tell me."

"Cecil Sears, a lawyer, here in Boston."

Felix said, "Jesus Christ, Cecil Sears? I met him three or four times, when we were still...when I lived in Boston. Isn't he up for some big judicial appointment or something?"

"Yes. That's him. Or was him. He's dead." She could hear Felix shuffling papers on his desk. She continued, "And his mother was Brooke Sears, who was murdered in Beacon Hill two weeks ago in an interrupted robbery."

"I'm sure the police are already all over this."

"Yes. But they don't know what to look for. I have to see you."

A silence, then Felix said, "How soon can you be here?"

"In fifteen minutes if I'm lucky, thirty if I'm not."

"Fine. I'll leave your name at reception. And hurry."

***

Fifteen minutes later Madeline breezed into the headquarters of *TheBoston Globe* in a high-rise office tower on State Street, its high vaulted ceiling like a cathedral she'd always thought. After she gave her name, she was handed an access barcode and skipping the elevator, took the stairs to the second floor. And on the way up almost bumped into the brown-haired model, Felix's date at the opera. Madeline would have said hello but the woman was looking down at her cell phone.

Madeline walked down the hall to Felix's office, his door wide open. He was on the phone, leaning back in his chair, feet up on his desk. No jacket, just the usual white shirt and blue jeans. He sat up and waved her in.

Felix hung up and said to her, "I just checked with our Metro guy, and he doesn't know anything about the shooter, but he did confirm that Cecil Sears was the victim. The police are looking for a black, late-model car with a Massachusetts license plate. By the way, there's at least a million of those in the state."

Madeline asked, "Where did it happen?"

"In the alley behind Old City Hall."

"And no witnesses?"

"They haven't found any who saw the shooter. Besides, it was pretty much dark by then. There were people in the alley, heading home after work, and they said they heard a 'bang' but thought it was a car backfiring. Then Cecil dropped to the ground and a couple people called 911."

Madeline shivered. "Do you think it was the Mafia?"

Felix shrugged, "I don't know, could be," and he picked up his phone, punched in a number, and hit the speakerphone.

A second later a man's voice said, "Commissioner's Office."

"Connect me to the Commissioner please. Tell him it's Felix Fassbinder."

A ten-second pause and a gruff voice came on the line, "Commissioner Maxwell."

Felix said, "I missed a lot of things about Boston after I left. Oddly enough Harry, you didn't make the list."

"Felix, you worthless son-of-a-bitch, I heard you were back. And you're already bugging me? Can't you just pretend I'm retired? Which I will be in two years if I don't die of a heart attack first. What do you want?"

"It's nice to hear the sound of your voice too."

"The feeling is not mutual. And I have no time for a 'Welcome Back' party for you, so if you're calling to invite me, I'm busy."

"I hear that Cecil Sears was just murdered."

"And how did you hear that?"

"Never mind. Just leave it that I know. What I don't know is who's so interested in knocking off the Sears family?"

"An interesting question isn't it? I'm surprised you don't know the answer, 'Mr. Big-Time Pulitzer Prize Winner'. Shouldn't you be out on the street, gathering information for a story? Oh wait, you're in charge of online bullshit or something at *The Globe* now aren't you?"

Felix said, "So Cecil Sears has just been murdered and I'm curious if there's anything new on the murder of his mother, a couple of weeks ago. And what's the connection to her son's murder? Sounds like a gang connection to me, the good old-fashioned kind of gang. So maybe it's the Mafia that's coming after the Sears's family."

"The Mob? Who's your source on that?" The Commissioner laughed, "I know, 'wild horses, etc.' Why are you asking about the Mafia? What do you know?"

"Nothing really. Just a hunch. But Harry, a mother and son from a prominent family in Boston have been murdered in less than two weeks right under your nose? Sounds like you're slipping."

"One was a home invasion, the other one, could have been a botched mugging...who knows...or could have been a pissed off client who got sent to jail. They do tend to get prickly when they're sent to the slammer I've heard. So what do you know? Spit it out."

"I was thinking there could be a link with the Barzetti family. You might want to check into it. And if there is a connection I…"

"The Barzetti's? They're long gone from Boston and good riddance, but that's an interesting twist. What kind of connection?"

"Well, I can't really say. I have no proof, just things I've heard. That the Barzetti's might be involved."

"You've gone soft in the head."

"Just check the family out, that's all. They were a nasty organization, and might have had a run with the Sears years ago. According to my source."

"So you don't have anything better to do than sit on your butt in your fancy office and come up with conspiracy theories about the Mafia from your trailer-trash sources?"

"I've always had better sources than you. And you know it."

A silence, then the Commissioner said, "Well, it's a waste of time. A guaranteed waste of time. You should have stayed in Chicago and done some reporting on their murder rate. Which is much worse than Boston's, by the way, and a national disgrace."

"So Harry, what suspects do you have for the Sears's murders? I'm curious who's killing off the Sears family. And I was wondering if you might have any information for me."

"So you're still a reporter? Don't hold your breath Felix. And if you have to call me again, make sure it's worth my while."

"Every time I've ever called you it's been worth your while."

"You flatter yourself. Anyway, I have to go catch me some bad guys," and the Commissioner hung up.

Felix turned and said to Madeline, "At least he'll have the Las Vegas Police Department check into it."

"But he said it was a waste of time and…"

Felix interrupted, "He always says that. I can tell you for sure he'll have two or three of his officers crawling all over Las Vegas checking on the Barzetti's. He cautioned her, "You can't ever tell anyone what I told you, about that old vendetta. I don't want Susan hauled in by the Boston cops for questioning."

"No worries. I won't. Although this whole thing does seem…like from a movie."

Felix laughed, "Where do you think the movie ideas come from? Real life that's where. But just don't talk about it."

Stung, she snapped, "Do you think I'm crazy? Of course I won't talk about it. But let me know the…"

"Boston Homicide is on it now. So be happy with that. Harry won't pass up the tidy tidbit I just dropped in his lap." He grimaced, "I'll have to stay on him though to get anything. He's a tight one when it comes to information. He's one of those cops who'd rather receive than give. But we'll see. Besides, the Barzetti angle might not even be a story." He looked at her and smiled, his 'hunter' smile, the way he smiled when he was on the trail of breaking news. She hadn't liked that smile when they had been married, and she didn't like it now.

What had she just done? Forget Pandora's Box, the whole story of Brooke's secret was about to burst out of a genie's bottle. And Felix was the man in the turban. The story would make Boston headlines, and roil the internet for months. She felt a stab of regret. Brooke would have hated the publicity, would have been shattered by it really, but she was dead now so it didn't matter. Madeline hesitated. But still it did matter. To her.

Madeline did know Paige wouldn't like the coverage. Although maybe she would. Paige seemed like a woman who reveled in the sensational. And maybe the Mob had their sights set on Paige too? Maybe they intended to take out the whole Sears family. And here she was poking around for rumors based on an old story, written by…who knew who really wrote the chapter "A Brahmin Slut"? And to make it worse, she was being all chummy with an ex-husband while the Sears family was literally dropping dead all around her.

She said to Felix, "You'll let me know right away when you hear back from the Commissioner?"

"Of course. If there's anything solid Harry will call me back, looking for my source. With his usual threats." He leaned forward in his chair, smiling at Madeline. "It's good to be back." She stood up and he stood as well. He said, "But Madeline, do be careful."

"I was born careful."

She didn't apologize for dragging him into a murder. He loved it, and this was how he made his living. Or at least how he used to make his living.

He leaned forward and kissed her on the cheek and she walked out the door.

Outside, she got in her car, not about to wait, yet again, for Felix to call her. There must be something she could do.

Alfred, she should talk to Alfred. She checked her watch; it was after 8:00. Late, but not too late. She pulled out her cell phone.

Alfred answered on the first ring, and she said, a statement rather than a question. "It's Madeline. You've heard about Cecil."

"Yes. I've spoken to Paige. A number times."

"I know it's late, but can I come and see you? I'd like to talk about Cecil."

"Yes, of course," and he gave Madeline his home address in Wellesley.

***

Madeline drove well over the speed limit all the way Alfred's, and finally pulled into his tree-lined driveway and drove up to a ghostly, white brick estate set well back from the street. Alfred walked outside to meet her once she parked behind his black Lexus, and he led her inside, through a foyer of tall potted palms and mirrors, a formal dining room, and then into his study. He clicked on the lights.

"This is not the time for coffee," he said, his face the usual shade of pale gray and walked to the bar. "Scotch?" he asked, and when Madeline nodded, he poured healthy slugs of Macallan 12 into two shot glasses and handed one to Madeline. Her cell phone rang and she clicked it on mute.

She began, "I was supposed to meet Cecil for a drink at the Parker House about a block from his office at 5:00 this afternoon," she said. "But he didn't show up. Now I know why."

Startled, Alfred said, "You saw it happen? You saw whoever it was shot Cecil?"

"No, I was downstairs in the bar when it happened. But when Cecil was a half hour late I went outside to look for him, and there were cops all over the street. They told me there'd been a shooting."

Alfred didn't reply, but downed the shot of scotch and slumped in a red leather chair behind his desk.

She asked, still standing, "How is Paige?"

"Paige is...Paige."

"What does that mean? I don't know her."

Alfred took a drink and leaned back, settling in his chair. "Paige is fine. Shocked of course, as we all are. But she's holding up."

"Does she think Cecil's murder is connected to Brooke's?"

"To Brooke's? She told me the police asked her about that. She doesn't know what to think. To be honest, Paige has never seen much beyond herself." He arched his eyebrows, "Why? Do you think there's a connection?"

"Yes, I do. But I'm curious what you think."

"What I think doesn't matter. It's what the police think that matters. I do know they have Paige under 24-hour guard now. Just in case." He added, "So what you and I talked about the other day, that story in the manuscript, well it's all immaterial. Now that Cecil is dead."

"So you don't think that story I showed you about Brooke and her Mafia lover has anything to do with Brooke's murder, and now Cecil's? To be honest, I think there's a good chance the Mafia gunned down Cecil."

"The Mafia? I hadn't thought about that. Seems a huge stretch, since that was a long time ago." Alfred stood up and poured himself another shot of scotch. He looked at Madeline and she shook her head 'no.'

Madeline asked, "Where is Paige?"

"She's staying with a cousin in the Back Bay. So you think the Mafia might have come after Brooke and then Cecil? Interesting. Have you mentioned any of this to the police?"

"I didn't, not directly, but I do know they are checking into it."

Alfred shifted in his chair. "Well, that's good to know."

"So did Cecil ever mention that he was worried about his safety?"

Alfred said, "So you're a homicide investigator now?" Madeline shrugged, and he continued, "I saw him about four or five days ago. And no, he didn't mention he was worried. But you say the police are investigating the Mob angle?"

Madeline nodded. Alfred's cell phone rang and he answered with, "Hello Paige." He listened for a minute and said, "I can be there in twenty minutes. Is there anything else you need?"

He disconnected and turned to Madeline. "That was Paige, and she wants to see me. Sorry, but I have to leave. Perhaps we can talk more in a day or so?" He pulled a thick file out of his desk, dropped it in his briefcase, and she followed him to the door. They walked to the driveway and she got in her car, did a U-turn, her headlights scanning across his massive hemlock trees, and drove down to the end of his driveway, Alfred's headlights right behind. She took a right and headed back to Boston.

Well, driving to see Alfred had been a total waste of time. But then he was more interested in the living. Madeline not so much.

***

Later, when Madeline drove down Medallion Ave. to the garage of her condo building, she saw a car idling in the dark, Detective Amick behind the wheel. Madeline pulled into a No Parking zone and walked over.

The detective got out of the car saying, "I need to talk to you. I have questions about Cecil Sears's death, since you were 'on-scene'. And by the way, none of my questions are related to Mrs. Sears's homicide, but of course you can have a lawyer present."

"No. It's fine. I can talk now. How can I help you?"

"I told you to wait for me earlier. In front of the Parker House after Cecil was shot. I was quite clear."

"I had to leave."

"You had information possibly relevant to a homicide investigation. I needed to talk to you. I've been trying to reach you on your cell phone."

"I already told you everything I know. Besides, I was five or six blocks away when the shooting happened, so I am hardly a witness."

The detective snapped, "I told you not to leave. But you did."

"Sorry. It won't happen again."

The detective glared at her. "About the reason for your meeting with Mr. Sears. What was it about?"

"I just wanted to talk to him about Brooke."

"About what specifically?" Madeline said nothing, and the detective continued, "I'd like to hear more about why you and Cecil were meeting. Who set it up?"

"I did. I called him and told him I wanted to talk to him about Brooke and the investigation into her murder. That's all."

"So why did Mr. Sears agree to meet with you? He told me he thought you were a 'nuisance'. That's what he said, 'a nuisance'. Were you aware of that?"

"Perhaps he found me a fascinating nuisance."

Her answer irked the detective, who scrawled something on a pad of paper and said, "So why didn't you just talk to Mr. Sears about the investigation on the phone? Why go to the bother of actually meeting?"

"Some conversations are just better in person."

"And who picked the place to meet?"

"I did."

"Why that particular place?"

Madeline shrugged. "It was close to his office. Convenient for him. And for me. My store is only about seven blocks away."

"And when did you have this telephone conversation with Mr. Sears?"

"After lunch. It lasted about a minute. I asked him if we could talk about Brooke's investigation since I hadn't heard anything, and..." Madeline was nothing if not quick on her feet, "and I suggested we meet at The Parker House this afternoon and he said fine. That was it. I was there at five, but when he wasn't there by five thirty, I went outside. And that's when I saw you."

"And no one knew you were meeting Cecil? Not even your business partner?"

"That is correct. Like I told you before, I didn't mention it to anyone. No one."

"Besides today, when was the last time you saw or spoke to Cecil?"

"At the reading of Brooke Sears's will. Paige was there too."

"When you learned she'd left you all of her jewelry? Likely not an amicable meeting."

"Given the circumstances, not exactly. You should talk to their estate attorney, Alfred Atkins about that."

The detective looked at Madeline, "Is there anything further you'd like to add?"

"No."

"Thank you. I'll be in touch tomorrow if I have any more questions. And by the way, don't leave town."

Detective Amick slid behind the wheel of her unmarked car and pulled away.

Madeline walked into her building, and the concierge at the front desk said, "There was a police officer here looking for you, a woman." He looked down at a paper on his desk. "A Detective Amick."

"Thanks, I just spoke to her outside. She's a bit of a bitch, but don't tell her I said that," said Madeline, and she took the elevator up to her condo.

***

Once inside, Madeline went to her study and checked her cell phone. Three calls from Detective Amick and two from Abby. She sent a quick text to Abby that she'd just gotten home and would call later. Drained, she stared out the window of her study at the Boston skyline. At least now, thanks to Felix, the police were going down the Mafia rat-hole and find whoever had murdered Brooke, and Cecil too most likely, and they'd be brought to justice.

She toasted Brooke silently, and then toasted her again, which pretty much finished her glass of wine. She called Abby, and they talked for half an hour about Cecil, Madeline not mentioning she'd been on her way to meet him because that would have added an hour to a conversation she didn't want to have.

As soon as she hung up her phone rang and the concierge said, "There is a Felix Fassbinder here to see you," and Madeline said to send him up.

152

She checked her watch, it was late, which probably meant he had good news. That's what she needed, good news on a very bad day. Two minutes later Felix knocked on her door.

Felix said, "I tried to call but I just got voice mail. I'm glad you're home."

"I just walked in the door. Do you want a glass of wine?"

"No. Coffee would be good."

She locked the door after him, threw the dead bolt and said, "So what's up?" and led him to her galley kitchen and put a pod in The Keurig machine. She poured a healthy glass of wine for herself.

He glanced into the living room, Chinese oriental rugs on the hardwood floor, brown leather furniture and a view of downtown Boston. "Nice place," he said as she led him into the dining room. "I see you kept the table we bought in Maine."

They had disagreed about the walnut table five years ago when they'd found it in a dim antique store in York, Maine. He said it looked like a medieval monk's writing desk and wanted it. She didn't. They bought it.

Felix slumped in a dining room chair then leaned forward, drumming his fingers on the walnut table. "Sorry, but I have bad news. I just talked to Harry, the police commissioner. He wanted to gloat."

"Gloat?"

"About the Barzetti lead. It's a non-starter. I'm afraid there's no story there, no Mafia story anyway. There is no Organized Crime connection to Brooke's murder, or Cecil's. None."

Madeline abruptly set down her glass of wine, hard enough that drops of chardonnay splashed on the table. She sat down. "What? What do you mean?"

"Like I told you, Davio Barzetti moved to Las Vegas after they rolled up their Boston operations and went legit. Harry just told me Davio died a year ago. Leukemia. Divorced, no kids, and no siblings. Which means there aren't any Barzetti's left. Well, there's a second cousin twice-removed, or something in California."

"Well, maybe he had Brooke..."

Felix shook his head. "That would be 'she'. The cousin is a girl. And she's sixteen and is in a boarding school in London." Felix sighed, "There's nobody else left, and all the old lieutenants from the Barzetti family have been dead for years. So the Boston cops are going after more viable leads. I'm guessing they're digging into Cecil's current caseload, and checking into his time as a prosecutor too. And knowing Harry, he'll have his Homicide people pouring through files, looking for an angry defendant who may have made threats against Cecil. As far as his mother's murder..." and Felix's voice trailed off.

Madeline said, "So the police do not think they're connected?"

"Correct. As of right now they're thinking *not* connected. That could change, but likely not. At least that's what Harry said."

"But what about Brooke?"

Felix stood and paced up and down her dining room. Cracking his knuckles as he walked, another old, annoying habit. "You know it would have been a great story," he said. "Even after all these years the Sears name still means something in Boston. And to have two family members murdered in a couple of weeks by the Mafia? Unbelievable. Of course I was interested in it, big-time, even though that's not what I do anymore. Unfortunately.

He continued, "It looks like Brooke's death was just a burglary gone wrong and Cecil was possibly murdered because of an old court case. I'm sure there is a story there, just not a Mafia one."

Madeline said, "So the police won't follow up on the organized crime angle? But..."

"I just told you, it's more or less a non-starter. According to Harry, this Davio was the soul of propriety once he moved west and went into real estate. Which means he died a rich, model citizen, and legitimate. Well, likely more or less legit. In Las Vegas nothing is totally legit."

Madeline set a cup of coffee in front of Felix. "But...but the police can't just ignore a possible connection to the Mob. And besides, in the old manuscript I told you about, the Barzetti family had Brooke's lover murdered in downtown Boston at rush hour. Just like Cecil. Hardly a coincidence. The police can't just drop the Barzetti lead."

Felix said, "They can. Anyway, I didn't want to tell you over the phone that your whole Mafia conspiracy theory has gone up in flames, like the

Hindenburg. So even if the story in this manuscript or whatever you have is true, the cops won't want to hear about it because it's not relevant to either of the Sears's murders."

Madeline stared at him.

He stood up. "Anyway, I'm really sorry Madeline, but there's nothing more I can do to help you. I tried. But whatever old story you're chasing…for whatever reason…it has nothing to do with murder. And it's a waste of time to go chasing after an old Mafia vendetta."

"What? But Felix, you can't just…"

"Madeline, I know you want to find out who murdered Brooke, and as an old reporter, so do I. And Cecil? Who knows? But it looks like neither one was Mob related. So just let it go." He stood up.

Madeline shook her head, "No, I'm not going to 'just let it go.'"

"Well, just because you want something to be true doesn't mean it is true."

"I'm sure the Mob was involved," she insisted, her voice rising.

"Well, the police think otherwise. And I'm telling you, you're wasting your time trying to pin it on the Barzetti's. Well, it has been interesting, or sort of interesting." He looked around her condo, "Anyway, I have to go and…"

"You're leaving? Now? You can't just walk away! You can't just walk out."

He jerked his head back to her, his face pale. "Oh really? You left me," and he snapped his fingers, "just like that. While I was out of the country, thousands of miles away."

"What? Why are you bringing that up now? I had no choice. Besides…"

Felix's blue eyes were smoky blue now. "Don't give me that. You had a choice. You moved out while I was away, on assignment. You couldn't even wait until I got back. And…"

"And who knew when that would be? And why should I have stayed? For what? You were gone most of the time. So there wasn't hardly any of you…for me." Her voice rose again, "And did I mention you hated to be home? It was like you wanted to be anywhere but home."

"Maybe that was because I had a wife who hated anything to do with Spotlight, or reporting. What reporter wouldn't want to be away? Look, we both made mistakes back then." He shoved his chair back and stood up.

Madeline turned on him, "Felix, we've had this conversation before. A number of times as I'm sure you recall. You make me sound like a harridan or something. Don't drag up the past. You know what, it doesn't matter anymore."

Felix didn't say anything in the cold silence, just stared at her, withdrawn. She'd seen that look before.

They had spoken only three times after she'd moved out, and Madeline was surprised that Felix had been surprised that she had been serious about divorcing him. After that, they communicated only through lawyers, and Felix hadn't even been at the last court hearing. His lawyer said he was back in Moscow, on assignment. Which might have been true, or not. For all she knew he was having an affair with a colleague

"You're right Madeline. None of that matters anymore." And Felix walked through the hallway and out the door. The click of the lock as it shut had a loud, final sound.

Madeline sat at their dining room table, unmoving. Well, this was one horrible day. Brooke's murder was still unsolved, and now Cecil was dead and God knows who murdered him. And Felix, well he was stuck in the past. And there was nothing she could do about any of it.

***

That night Madeline dreamed about Brooke.

In the dream, Brooke sat in Madeline's living room in the black calfskin chair by the fireplace, wearing a gray Versace caftan, a long strand of pearls around her neck, her ice-white hair pulled back with pearl combs. Madeline was in dark sweatpants and sneakers. In her dream they both knew Brooke was actually dead, although neither brought it up.

Brooke looked at Madeline and said, "You've let yourself go."

"I have?"

"Yes. Quite. Your hair..." and eyebrows furrowed, Brooke studied Madeline's blonde hair. "It needs a good cut." Her gaze slid down to Madeline's sweat pants. "And if I had a book of matches with me I'd set

156

those on fire. Your sneakers too."

"I'm relaxing."

Brooke sniffed.

"I miss you," said Madeline.

"Well, it's too bad, since there's nothing to be done about that. Too late, if you know what I mean."

"I am glad to see you," and Madeline almost asked her if she wanted coffee or anything, but caught herself in time. Brooke was dead.

Brooke said, "I just want to sit and talk. Like we used to."

"About anything in particular?"

"Well, we could talk about the Boston Patriots," and she laughed her low throaty laugh.

"The name is the New England Patriots."

"Whatever," said Brooke, and waved her right hand dismissively. The diamonds gone now of course.

Madeline woke up then, and it took her a second to realize it had been a dream. Just a dream. When she got out of bed at six, the dream was still fresh and vivid, and she walked into the living room and stared at the chair where Brooke had sat and told her all she wanted to do was talk.

Madeline wished she'd asked Brooke who had murdered her, but it wasn't that kind of dream. Nevertheless, the dream haunted her. The problem was there was nothing more Madeline could do to track down her murderer. The police would have to take care of that. And Capote's manuscript that she thought was such a powerful piece of evidence was just a story, an old, tattered, sad story. A story she was still convinced was true, but one that had no relevance now.

As she walked out of her living room Madeline decided that as a final, farewell to Brooke, and this time a truly final one, she'd go to Cecil's funeral. Brooke would appreciate the gesture. Madeline stopped and looked in the mirror. And yes, she did need a haircut.

She'd get one before Cecil's service.

Chapter 10

When Madeline told Abby the next day that she was going to Cecil's funeral, Abby didn't say anything, just rolled her eyes.

Two days later Madeline walked up the steps of Trinity Episcopal Church in the Back Bay, twenty minutes early for Cecil's funeral. Just in case. She didn't know in case of what, she just wanted to be there early. She took a seat in the back of the church, scanning the bereaved as they arrived. One of the first was Alfred, who strode up the aisle to the roped-off section in front for family. He looked to neither the right nor the left, but dressed in gray again, he marched forward, like an old soldier. Over the next fifteen minutes a crowd of well-dressed mourners streamed into the church, and Madeline recognized Boston's Mayor, as well as the governor of Massachusetts, and then a man with bushy black eyebrows she thought was a senator. Five minutes later, to thunderous organ music, Cecil's gleaming copper-colored casket, was wheeled up the aisle, followed by his weeping, red-haired wife and a stone-faced Paige in a long black cape and a tight black dress, her short dark hair slicked back. And behind them, a line of Sears relatives, all of them still rich.

Bishop Whiteman officiated at Cecil's funeral, and after the prayers of service, Paige went up to the lectern and spoke about her brother, who according to her had been a paragon of selfless virtue. Madeline wasn't buying it.

At the end of the service, Paige and Cecil's wife greeted the line of mourners in the vestibule. When Madeline walked up to them, the ubiquitous Alfred standing behind, looked up and nodded to her. Paige glanced briefly at

Madeline, her expression flat, and said, "It was good of you to come to my brother's funeral."

"My condolences. Brooke would have been heartsick. What a shock."

Paige said, over her shoulder, "Yes, it is a tragedy."

Madeline walked out of the cathedral and down the church steps, the grim hearse with Cecil's casket inside, idling at the bottom. She looked around but didn't see Detective Amick, then spotted her standing by the railing, her eyes raking the mourners.

Madeline checked Cecil's memorial card. The reception was at the Mandarin Oriental in the Back Bay, only a couple of blocks away. She might as well go to that too, after all it was close. And besides, this was her final, really final farewell to Brooke.

***

Fifteen minutes later Madeline walked into Cecil's reception on the third floor of the hotel, the mourners clustered around black-draped café tables scattered around the room. A line of tables stood against the back wall, heavy with platters of sandwiches and tureens of soup, a phalanx of servers weaving through the crowd with glasses of white and red wine.

She stood just inside the door for five minutes and then spotted Felix, sitting alone at a table near the back, in a dark blue Tom Ford suit, watching the mourners as they walked in. She knew it was Tom Ford because she'd given it to him their last Christmas together.

So why was he here?

Felix looked up when she walked over and sat down. She said, "Why are you here?" He didn't say anything, and she said, "To be honest, I'm surprised to see you. You didn't know Cecil. So why did you come?"

"It's nice to see you too," said Felix. "Just because you don't know someone doesn't mean you can't attend their funeral reception."

"And you came because...?"

He shrugged, "To see who shows up. In Boston, people like Cecil don't usually end up murdered. So I thought I'd come to the final gathering of his friends and family. And see what I could see."

Madeline said, not hiding her annoyance, "So you are looking for a disgruntled former client of his to show up, with what...a disgruntled smile that gives him, or her away?"

"Maybe. Maybe not." Felix looked away, studying the room. He muttered, "I don't know what to think. I'm not sure what happened," and he turned back to her, "But I'd like to know."

"Well, good luck with that," she said, and scanned the room, looking for Paige. Madeline wished Felix would just leave. He didn't belong here.

He pointed to Alfred sitting at a table off to the side, talking to one of the Sears relatives. "Isn't that the Sears's lawyer? I saw him on TV giving a statement to the press yesterday, on behalf of Cecil's sister. Something about the tragedy of a brilliant life cut short."

Madeline said, "Yes, that's him, their lawyer." Felix didn't say anything so she added, "I didn't know *The Globe* worked funeral receptions. Like it was a newspaper beat or something."

"Funny," said Felix, keeping his eyes on Alfred.

"But you're not a reporter at *The Globe*. I thought you were a digital editor or something?"

Felix ignored the question then turned to her. "By the way, that old manuscript with a story about Brooke? The one you read that got you started on your 'Big Quest for Justice'? That story. I'd like to read it." And he turned to her, his blue eyes hard. "Not just hear you tell me about it. I helped you out, and now I'm asking for a return favor. I want to read it. Just to wrap things up."

"No."

He said, "You didn't even stop to think about it, not for even a second. Why not?"

"Because it's private, which means it's none of your business."

If Felix had the slightest idea the manuscript might be Truman's lost novel there would be no holding him back. The problem with winning a Pulitzer is that it creates a need for a second.

Felix said, "I'm just asking if I can read it. That's all. Because now, well I confess, I'm curious."

"Why? You already said the Mafia had nothing to do with Brooke's murder, or Cecil's. So it's immaterial."

"I'd still like to see it."

"That won't happen."

Felix stood up, leaning towards her across the café table. "I think you're hiding something, and I'd like to know what it is. Why are you so involved with the Sears family? I want to know why it's so important to you? It's highly unusual to have two murders in a family like that in a little over three weeks but..." and his voice trailed off.

She shook her head. "I'm sure the police are finding it very odd. Why don't you ask them, since you're such good friends?"

Felix said, "You wanted help, my dear, or rather my ex-dear, and I tracked down the Barzetti info for you, which didn't turn out to be the answer, but still, I called in some favors for that. So you owe me."

"I owe you nothing. Well, all right, I owe you a thank you. I already told you thank you several times but I'll say it again. 'Thank you'. There, obligation over and done with. I'm good. Are you good?"

He said, his laugh bitter. "It wasn't all my fault you know. The divorce I mean."

She stared at him. "Why are we talking about that again? First of all, I don't want to talk about it. And second, I don't *ever* want to talk about it again."

Felix stood up, buttoning his jacket, not looking at her. "I think I should mingle with the grieving friends and relatives." And he walked off.

Madeline sat for five minutes staring after Felix. Then she made her way to the buffet, and when she turned around with a bowl of lobster chowder, Alfred was in line behind her.

Alfred said, "How good of you to come, Madeline."

"I came for Brooke."

A group of mourners walked into the reception and Madeline looked over. No Paige yet, but she was sure to show up any minute. Then Madeline could leave. She looked around but didn't see Felix, so he must have left. Good.

Alfred said, "It would have broken Brooke's heart that Cecil died so young…" and his voice trailed off. He picked up a ham sandwich, and when he turned back to Madeline, she pulled her black silk scarf to the side, so he could see Brooke's pearl and amethyst necklace tucked under it.

"It's Brooke's, one of the pieces she left me. I'm wearing it today in her memory. But I didn't want Paige to see it and be upset."

"That was thoughtful."

She put her hand on his arm, "Alfred, can you tell me why Brooke changed her mind and didn't leave her pearls to Paige? Why did she leave them to me?"

Alfred said, "I don't know. I can tell you that Brooke said more than once that you were a dear friend."

"She actually said that?"

Alfred's eyes glittered, "Yes. She also told me you were a pain in the ass, pardon my French. But I do know she trusted you."

"That was the reason she left me over three quarters of a million dollars' worth of jewelry? Doesn't that strike you as a bit strange?"

Alfred said with a half-smile, "You know as well as anyone that Brooke had a mind of her own."

Madeline sighed, "It still seems odd, but yes, Brooke always did exactly whatever she wanted. But Alfred, something must have happened a couple of months ago between Brooke and Paige. If Brooke were alive, she'd tell me." Which Madeline knew was not true, but she liked the way it sounded, and it might get Alfred to talk.

Alfred pursed his lips, and said after a hesitation. "Well, I can say there was a falling out between the two of them, but I don't know what it was about. And it would have been inappropriate for me to ask."

Madeline said, "Well, that's not exactly helpful."

Alfred sighed, "That's all I know. I do know that Brooke didn't approve of Paige's career, or rather she didn't approve of the movies that Paige made. Brooke said Paige was in love with blood, and that her movies were full of it, dripping or gushing or pooling, or whatever. I wouldn't know, since I never saw any of them. To be honest, I think Brooke would have been happier if Paige made pornographic films." And he smiled. "Anyway, I didn't have the sense they argued about Paige's career. It was about something else, but I don't know what that was. Sorry."

Alfred looked around, as if he wanted to end their conversation. Madeline didn't.

She asked, "Alfred, do you think Cecil was murdered by a former client?"

Alfred's eyes shifted uneasily. "Well it would seem so wouldn't it? Clients always blame the lawyer when their case is lost. Could be that one of them held a festering grievance."

"So you don't think that whoever killed Brooke might have killed Cecil?"

"No, I do not. Why would the thieves who murdered Brooke have a reason to murder Cecil too? I don't see any connection." He glanced to the door and said, "Well, it was good to see you. You know Madeline there is something I've been meaning to talk to you about. So maybe next week we can..."

Madeline interrupted, "Of course, but I can talk now," and she nodded to an empty table.

Alfred said, "Well, I guess this is fine," and they both sat down. "About the manuscript you showed me a week-and-a-half ago." He paused.

Madeline nodded.

"I've been meaning to ask when you found the manuscript. You said you found it at Brooke's?" Madeline froze as Alfred pressed on, "So you went to her townhouse, after she died, and..."

Since Madeline was nothing if not quick, she shrugged. "Did I? I misspoke. I wasn't thinking. The manuscript must have been in one of the boxes of papers she sent over to my condo the day she was killed. And it must have fallen out. Or something. That's where I found it. At my place. The police have already picked up all of her boxes. I imagine they'll turn them over to Paige now."

Alfred adjusted his glasses, watching her. "Misspoke? I...see. Regardless, my point is the manuscript you have does not legally belong to you. It belongs to Brooke's estate."

Madeline didn't say anything, and he continued, "Look, I know you want to protect Brooke's reputation. Let me assure you, I want to protect it as well. Regardless, I am the executor of her estate, and in that capacity, I have to insist that you turn the manuscript over to me. It should be in my possession until all of her estate issues are settled. I can come by your store in Downtown Crossing tomorrow afternoon, about three and pick it up."

Madeline looked at him. There was no way she was about to hand over Capote's manuscript to anyone. She said, "That won't work because I won't be at the store tomorrow. I have to be at a gem auction in Marlborough all day tomorrow." A quasi-lie. There was an auction, but Abby was going.

"You can leave it at your store with your business partner and I'll swing by and pick it up."

"Unfortunately, that won't work since I have to leave very early, before seven, and the manuscript is in my safe deposit box at the Bank of America." She was turning into quite the facile liar.

"Well then, can I pick it up the day after tomorrow? I do have to fulfill my responsibilities as executor you understand."

Madeline said nothing.

He continued, "I'll be in Boston for a court hearing so I can come by around two. That manuscript would be best with me. That is the law Madeline. If that doesn't work, I can stop by later in the afternoon if that would be better. How about four thirty?"

"Yes, I guess that will be fine." Yet another lie. She'd text him later and postpone that appointment as well. The good part was he didn't know where the manuscript was.

Alfred stood, "That works, so I'll see you day after tomorrow. He looked over at a big table of relatives and said to her, "Well, it was good to see you, and sorry, but I have to speak to some people."

Madeline watched Alfred cross the room and pull up a chair at the big table. There was no way she'd ever give him the manuscript. She had it and he didn't, and she meant to keep it that way for, well for forever.

Madeline turned so she could watch the front door and a minute later Paige walked in, standing for a moment framed in the doorway, unwinding the long, black scarf around her neck. Behind her was a uniformed police officer, his eyes sweeping the room.

Madeline watched Paige walk from table to table of mourners, not sitting down but stopping for hugs and conversation. Finally, Paige walked up to Madeline's table and a waiter stopped with a tray of glasses of white wine, and Paige lifted off two, downing the first.

Paige set the empty wine glass on Madeline's table and said, "Hello again," and sat down. Up close, Paige's kohl-rimmed eyes were flat. Bleak. Madeline checked her scarf, making sure it covered Brooke's pearl necklace.

"I was surprised to see so many people at Cecil's funeral," said Paige as she took a drink from her second glass of wine. "I'm still in shock that he's gone. I can't believe it." Another long pull from her wine glass and she said, "I'm flying back to Los Angeles the day after tomorrow, now that I…well, I have a lot of things to do.

"I've decided I'll never come back to Boston, not with Mother and now Cecil gone. Too many sad memories. I was thinking of shooting some scenes here, but now I just want to go home."

Relieved that Paige would be leaving Boston, Madeline said, "This has been a double tragedy for you. And I am sure Brooke would have been devastated by Cecil's death, if she were still alive. You know I saw her the day she died? She was so excited and happy. All she wanted to talk about was her book."

Paige took another long drink of wine and set the now empty glass on the table, and said, surprised. "Her book?"

Madeline said, "Yes, she'd just decided to write one. A book about the people she knew when she lived in Manhattan years ago." She smiled at Paige. "It would have been an interesting read. Very, very interesting". Madeline paused, "She talked to me about the remarkable people she knew back then."

The reception had become noisier as people said their goodbyes, so Madeline raised her voice, "Yes, Brooke lived quite the life years ago, didn't she? All those unusual people and their stories. It would have been a fascinating read." She smiled at Paige and ended, "I'm quite sure you know what I mean. Quite sure."

Paige just stared at Madeline for a long minute, and said, "Yes, I think I do know what you mean. Excuse me, but I have to have a word with Bishop Whiteman before he leaves," and she walked over to a crowded table by the door, where a waiter squeezed in a chair for her. And there was Felix, sitting beside Alfred at that table, the two men chatting away. About what? She thought Felix had left. What was he doing, pumping Alfred for information?

Madeline stood up. It was time for her to go. She was finally really and truly this time done with the Sears family.

Chapter 11

J ust after two the next day, Madeline was alone in the back of the store
when someone rang the buzzer in three demanding bursts, and she
looked out front. There stood Paige in a long black coat, a gloved finger
jabbing the buzzer, a black purse slung over her shoulder.

Why was she here?

Madeline walked out and opened the door for her. "Hello, Paige. Come in,
and again, my sympathies. Can I get you a cup of coffee? Or would you like
water?"

Paige said, "I was in the neighborhood and thought I'd stop by." Her eyes
slid across their glass jewelry cases, and turned back to Madeline. "Did I
mention yesterday that I fly to Los Angles tomorrow?" and she walked along
the front glass case, scanning the display of Brooke's pearls, and commented,
"Looks like you've sold a couple of Mother's pieces."

Madeline froze. "We have."

Paige fidgeted with her purse strap and stared at Madeline. "Yesterday you
said Mother told you about a book she was going to write. A book about
the years she lived in Manhattan. And you told me it would have been a
fascinating read, and something about the intriguing people she knew, and
their stories." Paige held Madeline's eyes, "And then you said something odd,
you said, 'I'm quite sure you know what I mean. Yes, I'm quite sure.'

Paige hesitated and then continued, "And now I'm curious. What exactly
were you getting at?"

Relieved that Paige hadn't come to talk about her mother's pearls, Madeline
said, "Just that she knew unusual people. Your mother was here you know, in

the morning, the day she was…the day she died. Like I told you, she couldn't stop talking about her book. She asked me to work on it with her."

Paige paced again along the front glass case, her eyes on her mother's pearls and said over her shoulder, "Cecil told me before Mother died the only thing she wanted to talk about was her book. About her life." A harsh laugh, and Paige looked up, "Funny, she never said anything about it to me. Don't you think it's odd that my mother would write a book? Cecil said she called it 'a memoir,' about the people she'd known."

Madeline shrugged, "Well yes, I was surprised. But I think that maybe she wanted to re-live those years. It sounded like she had quite the glamorous life in Manhattan."

"Yes, so it would seem. Over the years I picked up bits and pieces about those times." Paige's eyes drilled into Madeline. "And then a couple of days ago Cecil said you wanted to meet up with him to talk about Mother's murder investigation. You know my brother thought you were obsessed with our family." She stared at a row of Brooke's pearl necklaces and turned back to Madeline, twisting the strap of her purse. "So what exactly did you want to talk to him about? He said you sounded a bit desperate." She set her purse on the counter, wrapping and unwrapping the strap around her wrist. "I think I would like a cup of coffee. Black please."

Madeline watched Paige's eyes, sliding around the room and then back to her purse. Uneasy now, Madeline walked over to the coffee machine, slipped a pod in the brew basket, and hunted for a clean cup. Making conversation, she said, "I just wanted to connect with Cecil and find out how the investigation was going." She watched Paige out of the corner of her eye. Maybe this talk about Cecil was painful for her. So Madeline changed the subject. "Brooke told me that Truman Capote invited your parents to his Black & White Ball. You've probably heard of it? In 1966? It was quite a swank affair. And famous."

"Yes, I've read about that party. The whole thing sounded predictable, and if you want my opinion, boring. Full of old, boring people."

Madeline pulled a clean cup out of the dishwasher. "Did Brooke ever say anything about Capote?"

Paige looked up, "My mother knew a lot of famous people back then in New York. I remember she called him 'That snake,' a couple of times. I gather they were close friends. And then they weren't."

Madeline thought about Capote's manuscript, about the part where he called Brooke's secret love-child the 'First Born'. A curious, old-fashioned nickname Madeline thought when she'd first read his manuscript and never thought about it again, until now. Why didn't he just say, 'Baby Boy', or something?

And Madeline stopped dead as she hit the brew button on the coffee machine.

Unless, unless the baby hadn't been a baby boy, but a baby girl. After all, Capote hadn't said one way or the other, just the nickname 'First Born'. When Madeline read the story, she'd assumed the child was Cecil, Brooke's oldest child. However, had the wily Truman meant the baby was the first-born child of her Mafia lover? Which would mean their child together was not Cecil.

It was Paige.

A clever twist by Capote? Could it be? If true, well that changed everything.

Madeline watched the coffee stream into the cup in silence. Exactly how much did Paige know?

Paige walked up and stood beside her, and said, her tone friendly now. "So what did my mother tell you about this memoir or whatever that she was going to write?" Madeline just stared at her and Paige said, an edge to her voice now, "I asked you, what did Mother say? I want to know what she told you about her damn book."

Madeline said, "About her book? Nothing really. Except she thought it would be a best seller."

With a jagged laugh, Paige tugged on the shoulder strap of her bag again, her eyes shifting around the room. Madeline looked over to the door, wishing a customer, or anyone would show up. Paige continued, "Mother was right about that. Yes, it would sell like hotcakes wouldn't it. There's nothing like a scandal, even an old scandal. I think my mother was getting a bit dotty in her old age, ready to spill her tacky secret to anyone who would listen." Paige nodded toward the back room and said, "I don't see your partner, I forget her name. Is she here?"

A tendril of alarm snaked up Madeline's neck and she said, "Abby? She stepped out, but she'll be back any minute." If only that were true. Abby would not get back from the auction in Marlborough for another two hours, maybe three. And where was Paige's security cop? Shouldn't he be with her? Madeline glanced out their front door. The hallway was empty.

Madeline handed her a cup of steaming coffee, and Paige pulled off her gloves and laid them on the counter. "Yesterday you said mother's book would be very, very interesting. And something about it being a fascinating read. So it sounds like my mother told you her secret? I bet she talked about my father." Paige looked at her and grimaced. "Of course she did. What did she say about him? I'm curious to know what she said. So tell me. Now. I want to know what she told you."

In the tense silence Madeline went back to the coffee maker and made herself a cup for something to do. She said to Paige, not looking at her, and carefully choosing her words. "About your father? Nothing really. She mentioned him only once. She said he died in a car accident in New York years ago." Madeline glanced at the clock. Should she just tell Paige to leave? No, that would likely infuriate her.

Paige snapped, "Come on, give me a break, I don't mean Henry Sears," and Madeline turned as she continued, "You were quite Mother's little confidant at the end, weren't you? She told me she spent a lot of time here," and Paige glanced dismissively around the Coda Gems store. "She told you, I know she told you about my real father. I did begin to wonder over time you know, from little things she'd say. Every now and then she'd get a funny look in her eyes when I'd do something, and she'd say, 'Oh, that's so like your father,' and then she'd change the subject. I always had the feeling there was something I was missing. That there was a big secret. I didn't know the truth until three months ago, and I can tell now that you do too. You know the truth."

Madeline said, keeping her face blank, "Know what truth?"

Paige paced again along the front glass case now, her eyes fixed on Madeline. "You've heard the old saying 'Blood will tell'? I learned something when I was in the hospital three months ago, something impossible actually. Except it wasn't impossible, if one knew the truth. And when I confronted Mother, she didn't deny it. But she swore to me she'd never tell anyone. Ever. But I bet she didn't keep her word, did she? Then when Cecil called and told me about Mother's book, I knew, I just knew, that juicy tidbit would be in there. Hidden of course, but still there, because my mother wouldn't have been able to resist."

Paige walked back up close to Madeline. Too close. Madeline stepped back as Paige said, "Even if Mother didn't spell it out in her book, friends of hers would figure it out, and then the whole world would know her big secret, which was really my secret."

Madeline edged a foot closer to the front door. She glanced at Paige, who was watching her.

"Look, I told you Brooke said she wanted to write a book, but that's all she said. Well she did mention a couple of people like Truman Capote, and Leonard Bernstein. Andy Warhol too."

Paige said, with a harsh laugh, "Who cares about them? I think you know the truth. About me."

"You? Brooke never said a word about you...anything about you. Or Cecil either. Ever. Nothing."

"I find that hard to believe, in fact so hard that I don't believe it at all. I can tell she blabbed to you." Paige's eyes darted around the room now, and she shifted from one foot to the other, her voice rising. "I have to know what Mother told you about my father. Tell me. I have to know exactly. You said yesterday her book would have been very interesting. Funny, I should think it would have been fascinating."

Paige started pacing again around the perimeter of their three glass cases and Madeline's eyes shifted from her to the front door and back again. Paige continued, "You'll probably tell Alfred, won't you? If you haven't already. Yes, Alfred would get a kick out of that information. He'd love to totally ruin my life, but he can't now because I fired him over the phone on my way here. Now that I'm in charge. I bet he'll call any minute to tell you, since you're best friends now. I saw the two of you were chatting away at Cecil's

A WIDOW IN PEARLS

reception before I walked in. Like old pals."

"Alfred? I barely know him," and abruptly added, "I need a little cream in my coffee," and Madeline walked to their small refrigerator and opened it.

Paige stopped pacing now, her face pale as she rocked back and forth, "Mother's problem, well one of them, was that she talked too much. You're a bit like her, you know. Which means you'll talk too much too."

Madeline, careful to avoid direct eye contact with Paige, glanced out the front door. Still no one in the hall.

Watching her Paige said, "My babysitter cop isn't here. I ditched him six blocks away. It was pretty easy."

"I guess I'll have to run downstairs for cream. I'll only be gone a second."

Paige jammed her hand into her shoulder bag, for her cell phone Madeline thought, but when her hand jolted out, she wasn't holding a cell phone but a gun, a nasty-looking snub-nosed revolver. That she aimed at Madeline.

And Madeline thought of Abby's gun in her desk in the back room, which for all the good it would do Madeline, may as well have been miles away. Which meant that she would have to get out of this the old-fashioned way. Madeline said, her voice steady, "Paige, please put that away. Let's talk about this. I'm sure you'll...."

"Forget it. You do like to talk, don't you?" and she steadied her right hand with her left, her forefinger resting on the trigger. "Mother should never have left you her pearls, especially when I really needed them. I really did need them you know. But I don't need them anymore. Bye-bye Madeline. Cecil said you were nosey, and you know what? He was right and I...."

"Oh look, here's Abby," lied Madeline looking over Paige's shoulder to the door, and as Paige turned her head, Madeline flung her cup of coffee at the gun in Paige's hand. The coffee sloshed onto the carpet as the china cup smacked against Paige's wrist. And with a huge boom and a thick smell of cordite the gun went off and Paige was knocked to the floor.

Paige moaned as a rush of blood from her upper arm seeped into the carpet and Madeline pulled off the scarf around her neck and tied a hard tourniquet around Paige's arm. Where was the gun? She heard a hammering on the front door and looked up. A cop, Paige's security detail? Yes, thank God. He

172

stood on the other side, weapon drawn. And she ran to the door to let him in.

Paige's eyes were closed as the cop checked her pulse and radioed for an ambulance and backup. He tightened the tourniquet and shouted at an ashen Madeline, "What happened?"

Madeline said, "Paige pulled a gun on me. I knocked it out of her hand and it went off."

His eyes jerked around, "Where is it?"

"I don't know. Maybe it's under her?"

"Anyone else here?"

She shook her head no, and his service pistol still in his right hand he patted her down with his left and ran to check the back office and the two closets. Madeline knelt beside Paige, her eyes still closed.

She said to Paige, "You're going to be alright. Don't worry…" and stopped. Madeline stood up. Screw that. This woman had meant to kill her.

The cop ran back to Paige, moving slightly on the floor now and took her pulse again.

And then the questions started. How did she know Paige, why was Paige at the store, and why did she pull a gun on her? Madeline told him how she knew her, and what had happened, but the cop was still suspicious, not letting go of his gun.

Five long minutes later two cops showed up, and five minutes after that three EMT's blasted in, lifted Paige onto a stretcher and wheeled her out the door and around the corner to the elevator. They hadn't touched the pistol that had been lying under her, the muzzle pointing uselessly at the front door. One of the officers bagged it.

The other cop locked the door, made Madeline sit in a chair, and a string of questions began. Later, Madeline wasn't sure how much later, there was more hammering on the glass door and Detective Amick was let in, followed by a forensics team, all cameras and clanging equipment, and the detective huddled with the other officers. Then Detective Amick ordered one of the forensics guys to swab Madeline's hands, and to send someone to the hospital and swab Paige's as well. Madeline watched as the photographer walked around the store snapping crime scene photos.

Detective Amick said to Paige's security detail, "I'll handle the witness," and turned to Madeline, patting her down again as she said, "You. Again. Every time you're around a Sears family member they end up dead or wounded. You're coming down to headquarters with me. As in now. Call your lawyer and have her or him, meet us there."

Madeline's hand shook as she dialed Anthony's office, and when he answered she said in a rush of words, "It's Madeline Lane. There's been a shooting at my store, and I'm being taken to the Boston police headquarters. Come as soon as you can."

"Fine. But don't say anything until I get there," and he hung up.

Then more banging on the front door and Madeline looked over, a distraught Abby peering through the glass saw Madeline, and motioned her over. Detective Amick shouted at Madeline, "How the hell did she get on this floor? This is a crime scene for God's sake." The detective snapped at Paige's security detail, talking on his cell phone, "Get rid of that woman at the door."

But Madeline got to the door first and opened it a crack.

Abby said, "My God, what's happened? Are you all alright?"

"I'm fine. But they won't let you come in."

"Thank God you're alright." Abby added, sotto voice, "You didn't..."

Madeline shook her head. "No, I didn't. Paige pulled a gun on me, and it went off. I'm being taken to headquarters." She said to the security detail as he walked up. "Talk to Abby Lane, my business partner. She'll have to stay here and lock up. By the way, she knows Paige."

Detective Amick walked over to Madeline, "Alright, let's go," and the two of them walked out, past a pale-faced Abby, and once outside went up to a blinking police car pulled up on the sidewalk. Madeline slid into the back seat as if it was a taxi and stared out the window at the curious passersby.

***

At police headquarters Detective Amick took Madeline's cell phone as usual, and directed her to an interview room, and while they waited for her lawyer to arrive Madeline asked the detective, "How is Paige?"

The detective said, "In surgery. Her gunshot wound is apparently not life-threatening."

Madeline sat, waiting for her lawyer. Thinking about Paige. Twenty minutes later Anthony walked in, calm, authoritative and worth every exorbitant penny he was likely to charge.

Detective Amick held Madeline at headquarters for more than two hours that afternoon while she explained that Paige had showed up, became increasingly erratic and had pulled a gun on her, which Madeline had knocked out of her hand and it accidentally went off.

What Madeline told them was all true. Except she didn't tell them everything.

She had to concentrate to keep her story straight for Detective Amick and a second detective who'd walked in shortly after the interview began. Madeline went over Paige's unexpected visit to the store, and repeated their conversation, but didn't repeat anything Paige had said about her father. After Madeline finished the questions began, with her lawyer interrupting from time to time with a cautionary, "Don't answer that."

When Madeline got to the part where Paige had said she'd talked to Cecil the afternoon he was murdered, and that Cecil had told her he was meeting Madeline at the Parker House at five, Madeline was careful to keep her face blank, but saw Detective Amick and the second detective exchange sharp glances. And they had her repeat it.

Detective Amick asked, "This conversation between Paige and Cecil, was it by phone or in person?"

"She didn't say."

Not long after, a young cop walked in and handed Detective Amick a report that she read and said to Madeline's lawyer, "The swab of Ms. Lane's hands did not show traces of gunpowder residue."

Anthony smiled, "Excellent. So she should now be free to leave once she and I have reviewed her statement."

"So then the swab of Paige's hand did show gunpowder residue?" Madeline asked the detective, who didn't answer.

Thirty minutes later, after Madeline signed her statement, Detective Amick stood up and walked Madeline and her lawyer to the lobby.

After her lawyer went out the front door Madeline said to the detective, "I have just one more thing I'd like to add. About Paige."

The detective stared at her, waiting.

"I know you'll be taking a good, hard look at Paige's alibi for this afternoon. However, I know Paige was desperate for money, and I also know that according to the terms of the Sears's trust, the surviving sibling inherits the other's share of the annual dividends. Which is about three million dollars a year."

The detective fiddled with her badge, "Anything else?"

"No, that's it."

Detective Amick glared at her, and Madeline turned away and walked up to Abby, waiting on the big wooden bench, and the two partners headed out to the parking lot.

Once outside Abby said, "You obviously weren't charged with anything."

"Correct." Madeline said with a shadow of a smile.

"And how is Paige?"

"She'll apparently recover."

"Well, I'm driving you home so you can pick up some things, and then you're spending the night at my place. You don't have a choice. I insist."

Madeline didn't protest as Abby drove to her condo, where she threw a change of clothes in an overnight bag and they headed to Abby's house in Cambridge. On the long drive she told Abby what had happened in the store. The whole truth this time. That Henry Sears was Cecil's father, but not Paige's. And why Paige had pulled a gun on her.

"You could have been killed," Abby commented at least five times.

Madeline finally said, "Stop saying that," and was silent for the rest of the drive to Abby's. Thinking. She needed to talk to Alfred.

***

Abby lived off secluded Buckingham Street in Cambridge in a restored two-story Queen Ann that Abby once said cost more to maintain than a bad gambling habit. The first thing Madeline did when she walked into the hall was call Alfred.

She told him Paige had pulled a gun on her at the store, and was accidentally shot by her own gun, but not critically, and was in the hospital.

"What? What? Where is she?"

"Massachusetts General. But Alfred I have a few questions about Paige."

Alfred cleared his throat, "I am bound by the rule of attorney-client privilege, but that being said, I can't believe Paige pulled a gun on you," and then he added, "Alright, I can. But why? About the pearls?"

"That was part of it. But Alfred, you said Paige is fascinated with blood?"

"Well, yes, she does seem to be. Why?"

"I thought you might know if Brooke ever said anything about Paige asking for her blood type, Henry's too, fairly recently. I know it sounds odd, but I thought I'd check with you. I don't know what she would have told Brooke, but it must have been good because..."

"How did you know? Paige got Brooke's as well as Henry's blood types from me, and I can tell you that because she asked for it, not in my legal capacity, but as a family friend. She called me from LA three months ago when she was in the hospital, right before Brooke flew out to Los Angeles. Anyway, Paige said she was doing some kind of online ancestry chart as a surprise for Brooke, and she needed her parents' blood types for a form she said they required. I had to dig for that information but I found it, in an old medical file."

"Does the file include Paige's blood type too?"

"Yes."

"So you have blood types for all three then. Good. Alfred, I need to know what their blood types are. It's important."

"Madeline, this is highly irregular. That is confidential information."

"I know, but two of them are dead. And Alfred, just remember that Brooke did trust me. All I can say now is that it's 'possibly' very important. And don't mention this to anyone, including Paige. Or the police. Could you please call me back with that info as soon as possible? Tonight? I'll explain later. And thanks."

Madeline hung up and Abby, standing beside her said, "Blood types? Why? What is going on?"

"Just an idea. A weird one. But everything fits."

Abby said, "At least it doesn't have anything to do with that damn manuscript you've been so obsessed with."

Madeline shrugged.

Ten minutes later Alfred called back. "Alright, I have the info, so grab a pen."

"Go ahead."

"The blood type info is Brooke: **B**+; Henry: **O**-; Paige: **AB**+."

"Got it, and thanks Alfred for getting back to me so quickly. I'll call you back and let you know if this is relevant. Promise. Sorry, I have to go."

"But I do need to know what…" but Madeline hung up.

***

At Abby's desk Madeline went online and printed off a blood type chart, checked it against Alfred's information, made notes and drew her own quick chart.

Abby said, looking over Madeline's shoulder, "What on earth are you doing?"

"Figuring everything out."

Abby headed to the kitchen and came back with a glass of wine for Madeline, who took a long drink and slumped in her chair.

"Alright," said Madeline, "I don't think Paige knew anything about Capote's manuscript, much less ever read it. But like I told you, she did suspect that Henry Sears was not her father, and one way to possibly find out was to compare Brook's and Henry's blood types to hers." Madeline pointed to the blood type chart, "And once she did, Paige knew for sure Henry Sears could not be her father. Impossible actually."

Abby stared at her, open-mouthed, "So what Paige told you this afternoon

178

was true?"

Madeline said. "How much do you know about blood types?"

Abby smiled. "It's been awhile, but I do remember a bit from college, and that blood type is inherited, just like eye or hair color. And that everyone has an **ABO** blood type, **A**, **B**, **AB** or **O**, as well as an Rh factor that is positive or negative, also inherited from the parents." Abby continued, "There's a lot more of course, but I don't remember it."

Madeline picked up her chart, "So two parents with a **B** blood type can produce a child with either **B** or **O** blood type. And one parent with **A** and another parent with **B** can produce a child with **A**, **B**, **AB** or **O** blood types. And finally, if one parent has **A** and another has **AB**, they can either produce a child with **A**, **B** or **AB** blood types."

Abby shrugged her shoulders. "Well it's as complicated as I remember. But why is it important?"

Madeline showed Abby the quick chart she'd drawn. "Henry's blood type was **O-** and Brooke's was **B+**; and Paige is **AB+**. So either Brooke was not Paige's mother, and I don't think there's any question there, or…Henry Sears could not possibly be Paige's father."

"You're sure about this?"

"Absolutely. So with the blood type information, Paige knew for sure her father was someone other than Henry Sears."

"But what about DNA? If Paige was so hell bent on establishing paternity, why didn't she go the DNA route?"

"Because Henry died years ago, and exhuming his body under any circumstances would have been a long, legal nightmare. More important though, Paige wouldn't want the world to know there was any question about her paternity, because she was one of the beneficiaries of Henry Sears's $200 million dollar trust fund. With the surviving sibling to inherit the other's.

Madeline continued, "So I'm guessing Paige decided to murder Cecil, so that she'd be the sole beneficiary. And besides, if she didn't kill him, she'd always have to worry that he might somehow learn she was not Henry's daughter, and get her kicked off the trust."

"So Paige killed Cecil."

"Well, yes. But first she murdered Brooke."

"Brooke?"

Madeline nodded, "Yes. I'm also guessing that Paige confronted her mother with the blood-type evidence when Brooke flew out to Los Angeles to see her a couple of months ago. Alfred knew Paige had a nasty argument with her mother when she was there, but he didn't know what it was about. I think that's the reason Brooke changed her will and left her pearls to me."

Abby said, "Oh my God Madeline. You need to go back to the police station right now, with the manuscript. Tonight. I'll drive you. We should leave now."

Madeline shoved the blood type charts into a file folder. "No Abby, I'm going to wait. I'm sure the cops now suspect that Paige murdered Cecil. And, eventually, their attention will shift to Paige in Brooke's murder investigation as well. But in that case the manuscript is only motive, not proof. Anyway, the police don't need the manuscript to charge Paige for Cecil's murder.

"And at some point, I'm sure the police will take Paige's Los Angeles alibi apart for the night of Brooke's murder, and I'm pretty sure they'll find a big hole. And she'll become their Prime Suspect. At some point. I think."

"But surely you care about justice?"

"I don't want Paige's true paternity to be made public unless it absolutely has to. Brooke would hate it. She was a very private woman."

"Brooke is dead," said Abby. "So it doesn't matter."

"It matters to me."

Madeline sent Alfred a text that the blood type information was not all that helpful after all. She knew he'd go to the police in a heartbeat if she told him the truth.

She hugged Abby goodnight and went upstairs to the guest bedroom, but didn't get undressed, she just lay on the bed, staring out the window at the bare Cambridge trees and went over a long list of "If onlys."

***

The doorbell rang at seven the next morning, and Madeline heard Abby slip down the stairs, then a mumble of voices in the foyer, and a minute later Abby knocked on the bedroom door and walked in. "Felix is here. Downstairs."

Madeline pulled the covers up tight around her. "Here? What does he want?"

"To see you."

"Whatever for?"

"I have no idea. He is quite insistent though. I told him you were asleep, but he said it was time you got up. I should go check on the store and have cleaners come in. The blood you know. There is a pot of coffee in the kitchen, and bagels and cream cheese on the side board if you feel like breakfast. I'll be back as soon as I can."

Madeline didn't respond, and Abby said, "I can tell Felix you're still asleep."

"No, it's fine," Madeline sighed and struggled to her feet, still in her jeans and sweater from yesterday.

"Nice pajamas you've got there," said Abby, and Madeline smiled and padded down the stairs.

Felix, standing in the front hall looked up and she said, "How did you know I was here?"

"I heard there'd been a shooting at Coda Gems, and when I knew you weren't the victim I went by your place but you weren't there. So I figured you might be at Abby's, and *voila*, I was right. You know Madeline I'd hate to have you end up on a mortuary slab without me ever getting a "'Proper Welcome Back' from you."

"What is a 'Proper Welcome Back'?"

"Use your imagination."

"Oh. I have a headache."

He laughed, and reached out and touched her shoulder.

She stepped back and said, "So you know what happened?"

"I know part of what happened. I thought maybe you could fill in the blanks."

"Paige has a streak of violence."

Felix said, "So Alfred told me."

"So that's what you were talking to him about at Cecil's funeral reception?"

"That, among other things."

"Will you write about it?"

Felix laughed, "No, I'm not a reporter anymore. I do miss it though. I really do miss it."

"So why are you involved?"

Felix ignored her question. "You know what, I actually thought Alfred might have murdered Cecil..."

"Paige murdered Cecil," Said Madeline, her voice flat.

"Now why didn't I think of that? Actually, I did. But you are fine? No bullet holes I should know about?"

"I appreciate your concern, and thank you for stopping by."

Madeline turned to go back upstairs and Felix put his hand on her arm, "I just wish that..."

"We all have wishes. I have to go," She said, stepping back.

Felix sighed and said, "Fine then. After all, tomorrow is another day," and leaned forward as if to kiss her on the cheek, but then turned and went down the front steps.

Madeline went back upstairs to bed. She wanted to sleep for about a year, but a couple of hours would do for now.

***

The next day Paige was charged with assault against Madeline, but that news was dwarfed by the media coverage the day after, when an eyewitness to Cecil's murder came forward. The woman, a Statistics PhD candidate at Boson University, said she had seen a woman who fitted Paige's description behind the wheel of a black Mercedes driving down the alley. And she saw the driver point a gun through the driver's side window at Cecil, and had memorized the license plate number.

Two weeks later the charge against Paige was murder in the first degree.

Madeline followed *The Globe's* intense media coverage over the next weeks, and Felix's name was not on any of the by-lines. So it looked like he really was no longer an investigative reporter. She was glad for that.

***

During the second month of Paige's sensational murder trial, Madeline and Abby opened Coda Gems' at their upscale new location, 18 Newbury Street, just half a block from the Boston Public Garden. It was a prime first-floor space, with 12-foot high windows, a loft in the back, and enough room for six glass jewelry cases to showcase their merchandise from Cartier, Tiffany and Bulgari, as well as collections by Gurhan and Liz Schuvart.

On their opening day, Felix came by with a bouquet of roses for Madeline, which she thought was sweet, but had no time to talk, other than to say a quick "thank you," and give him a kiss on the cheek. The two partners sold over $250,000 of jewelry that first day, and they couldn't stop smiling.

The next afternoon Detective Amick called and asked if she could come by Madeline's that evening.

"I wanted to let you know, in person," when she walked into Madeline's condo at seven that night. "We have a suspect in Brooke's murder."

"So you're looking at Paige?"

The detective nodded.

"Well, I hope your investigation leads to a murder charge."

"We'll see. There are…difficulties. We have no proof Paige was in Boston the night of Mrs. Sears's murder."

Then they talked about Paige's trial for Cecil's murder for ten minutes, with closing arguments at least a month away, and the detective ended, "I also wanted to let you know that in six weeks I'm transferring out of Homicide to Special Ops. A promotion. Which means you can always call me if you ever need anything," and the detective smiled, "like if you ever want a SWAT team to break down someone's door." It was a thin smile, but a smile nonetheless. A real one. The detective added, "That was a joke."

"I know."

Madeline walked the officer down to the lobby and at the front door the two women shook hands and the detective left for her unmarked car. As the detective drove off down the street, she turned on her siren for a split second as a goodbye, and Madeline laughed.

***

On the second day of the jury's deliberations in Paige's murder trial, Felix called Madeline at the store and told her to get down to the courthouse; the jury was coming in with a verdict. She ran outside and flagged down a cab, and when it pulled up to the Suffolk County courthouse Felix was standing on the bottom step, waiting for her.

They sat on a bench in the back and watched Paige walk to the defendant's table, minimal eye make-up, in a slim, long-sleeved black dress, no jewelry. The full courtroom fell silent when the jury filed in and took their seats, and their unanimous decision was delivered in a monotone, "Guilty of Murder in the First Degree."

No gasps from the courtroom. No one was surprised. Paige looked over, caught Madeline's eye and sneered.

Madeline and Felix left the courtroom and walked down the street to a Chinese restaurant a block away.

After they ordered, Felix said, "You realize Paige will get life without parole."

"I know. I am counting on it."

"You will never tell me what you know about this case, will you?"

"No, I can't. Sorry."

Felix shrugged, "Well, the Sears murders are still a big story. But I somehow have the feeling it could have been a blockbuster one, if I only knew all of it." And he laughed.

Madeline almost told him, "It would have been the story of a lifetime," but for once held her tongue. No sense in torturing Felix.

***

The next morning Madeline pulled Capote's manuscript out of the safe and told Abby, "There's something I need to do. I'll be back in an hour. Or so."

She drove home, and once inside dropped the manuscript on the kitchen counter. She stared at it, beat up, yellowed, and innocuous, and she thought

184

about her friend Brooke, who had for so long held onto a manuscript that was not so much a literary farewell by its author as a literary dose of poison.

The manuscript had not belonged to Brooke, and it certainly did not belong to her, but there was no way its brutal telling of old secrets should ever be published. Madeline scattered the pages of *Answered Prayers* in her fireplace, and opened the flue. She hadn't been able to stop Brooke's murder, or Cecil's. But she could and would stop this book from ever being published, now that she knew Paige was going to prison for the rest of her life. It wouldn't matter then if she was ever charged and found guilty of Brooke's murder—since a second life sentence would be meaningless.

Madeline struck a match, and she set the pages of Capote's magnum opus on fire. She could almost hear Brooke saying, her elegant eyebrows arched, "Yes, I suppose this is for the best." Madeline watched the flames lick through the pages until the most famously lost manuscript of the twentieth century was nothing but a pile of fragile ash.

***

A week later Abby sold Brooke's pearl and diamond pendant necklace to a wealthy stockbroker from Connecticut, the woman in beige who'd been to look at it months before. As soon as the wire transfer for $170,000 hit Coda Gems's bank, Madeline called the Truman Capote Literary Trust, a non-profit he established before his death to grant creative writing fellowships, and she asked to speak to the president.

Madeline explained that a deceased customer had known Truman years ago. "And I have a debt of honor that I have to fulfill. I am ready to wire a $170,000 donation to your non-profit, but for reasons of confidentiality, you cannot list my name. This donation must be listed as 'Anonymous' in your annual report."

The man asked her three times, "Is this a joke?"

"No. This is definitely not a joke."

Madeline's wire transfer was received by the non-profit several hours later, and the president called her back. Full of apologies, and questions. But

Madeline told him nothing more.

***

Madeline had lunch with Felix a week later, and he told her his 'sources' had said Paige's assistant, who had initially corroborated her alibi that she'd been with him at an all-day meeting in Los Angeles the day of Brooke's murder, said later he'd been confused, and changed his story. But according to Felix the police couldn't prove Paige had been in Boston the day Brooke was murdered, even though they did theorize she could have flown in and out from a private airport, or flown commercial under a false name. Either way, they had no proof.

Madeline was relieved, but careful not to show it.

After they ordered lunch Felix said, "You know I am glad to see you."

Madeline smiled, and said, "I'm glad to see you too."

"So maybe we could go out to dinner sometime. Not lunch, but dinner. At night. When it's dark outside." Felix grinned, "We always did have a lot to talk about. And now, well now I know you have a talent for crime."

"You mean committing it, or solving it?" she said, as a joke.

"Both. Since I know what you did."

She didn't look up from the slice of French bread she was buttering. "What do you mean?'

Felix laughed, "I've seen a bad, grainy and may I say poorly-lit security camera video from Brooke's townhouse. Of course I know how you walk. I would know that walk anywhere. It was you. It was definitely you. I'm an investigative reporter after all. That's what I do. Or did." A pause, "I guess it's still a part of me. So I'm curious, what in God's name were you doing there that night?"

Madeline was careful not to show any reaction. How could he have possibly seen that video? His damn sources no doubt. But how did they get their hands on it? Maybe the police took it from Cecil's home when they were collecting evidence after his murder? Possibly. Probably. But all she said was, "Felix, you don't know as much as you think you know."

186

Felix hesitated, then smiled, "Well, that could be true."

So he didn't know. Not for sure.

After lunch they walked out to the sidewalk, and he kissed her goodbye on the cheek, but this time added a kiss on the lips. And headed off down the street.

***

Over the next month Detective Amick called her every now and then about Brooke's murder investigation. The third time she told Madeline, "You know what, I miss working in Homicide. Maybe I've made a mistake. The Superintendent told me I can always come back. I can come back anytime, that's what he said." The detective continued, "You know what else he told me? He said Paige might never be indicted for Brooke's murder."

Madeline said, "To be honest, it's for the best this way. Really. Paige already has a life sentence with no possibility of parole for Cecil's murder, so justice has been served. No need to hammer it to pieces."

Which was true. But Madeline didn't want any more legal scrutiny of Paige, especially if blood type charts somehow surfaced that needed to be explained. That was all in the past, and should stay there. So Brooke could rest in peace.

"So you don't want to see Paige tried for Brooke's murder? That makes me curious."

"Well, it's a curious case."

"Someday you'll tell me what you know."

Madeline shrugged, "For me it's over, it's well and truly over."

"So why did Mrs. Sears leave her pearls to you? At least tell me that."

"Because she knew."

Detective Amick asked, "Knew what?"

"That I was a good friend."

"A good friend?"

"Yes. A true-blue friend. Big-time."

187

Acknowledgements

I would first like to thank Mary Buckham, for her brilliance and unrelenting good humor. And thanks as well to the Level Best Publishers, Verena Rose and Shawn Reilly, who love the thrill of a good story. And I thank Liz Schuvart for her knowledge of gemstones, Becca Hernan for her expertise in genetics, and to Susan Speakman, who knows everything about anything worth knowing. And finally, to my sisters, Marlene Stibal Talbot and Ann Stibal Lammers, who never bother to keep their opinions to themselves.

About the Author

Mary Stibal has never considered 'less is more' a virtue, especially when it comes to gems. (Think Mrs. Simpson.) She has also long known that beautiful gems are a stone-cold motive for any manner of crime. Especially murder. So using her decades-long business background, Mary weaves the deadly confluence of Boston's super-rich and their iconic jewels with deadly ambition and capital murder into a new series, "The Gemstone Mysteries."

Photo by Lori A. Magno

CPSIA information can be obtained
at www.ICGtesting.com
Printed in the USA
BVHW081021150320
575060BV00001B/110